Devil Tobiichi

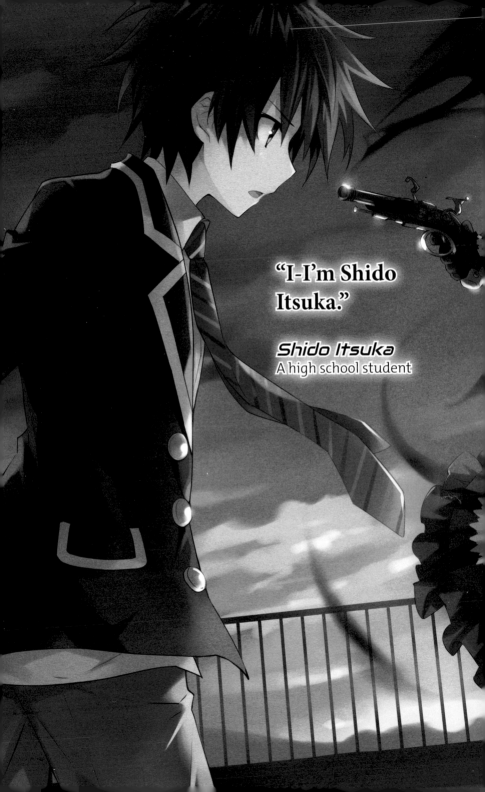

"I-I'm Shido
Itsuka."

Shido Itsuka
A high school student

"Aah, I didn't catch your name. Would you mind?"

Kurumi
A Spirit

"Oh. It's just, you know… when I thought about it, it was too embarrassing, like I'd feel, you know, stupid…"

Natsumi
A Spirit

"K-Kotori...
Calm down..."

Yoshino
A Spirit

"Natsumi!
Why are
you not in a
swimsuit?!"

Kotori Itsuka
Ratatoskr Commander

"I'm sorry if I upset you, Itsuka. I just had a bit of a shock because you look exactly like someone I met a long time ago."

Origami Tobiichi
Shido's Classmate

CONTENTS

"D-don't get the
wrong idea! I just…
This is—!"

Date A Live
Devil Tobiichi

11

Koushi Tachibana

Illustrated by
Tsunako

YEN ON

New York

Koushi Tachibana

Translation by Jocelyne Allen
Cover art by Tsunako

DATE A LIVE Vol.11 DEVIL TOBIICHI
©Koushi Tachibana, Tsunako 2014
First published in Japan in 2014 by KADOKAWA CORPORATION, Tokyo.
English translation rights arranged with KADOKAWA CORPORATION, Tokyo, through TUTTLE-MORI AGENCY, Inc., Tokyo.

English translation © 2024 by Yen Press, LLC

Yen On
150 West 30th Street, 19th Floor
New York, NY 10001

Visit us at yenpress.com
facebook.com/yenpress
twitter.com/yenpress
yenpress.tumblr.com
instagram.com/yenpress

First Yen On Edition: February 2024

Edited by Yen On Editorial: Ivan Liang
Designed by Yen Press Design: Jane Sohn, Andy Swist

Yen On is an imprint of Yen Press, LLC.
The Yen On name and logo are trademarks of Yen Press, LLC.

Library of Congress Cataloging-in-Publication Data
Names: Tachibana, Koushi, 1986– author. | Tsunako, illustrator. | Allen, Jocelyne, 1974– translator.
Title: Date a live / Koushi Tachibana ; illustration by Tsunako ; translation by Jocelyne Allen.
Other titles: Dēto a raibu. English
Description: First Yen On edition. | New York, NY : Yen On, 2021–
Identifiers: LCCN 2020054696 | ISBN 9781975319915 (v. 1 ; trade paperback) |
     ISBN 9781975319939 (v. 2 ; trade paperback) | ISBN 9781975319953 (v. 3 ; trade paperback) |
     ISBN 9781975319977 (v. 4 ; trade paperback) | ISBN 9781975319991 (v. 5 ; trade paperback) |
     ISBN 9781975320010 (v. 6 ; trade paperback) | ISBN 9781975348298 (v. 7 ; trade paperback) |
     ISBN 9781975349943 (v. 8 ; trade paperback) | ISBN 9781975350307 (v. 9 ; trade paperback) |
     ISBN 9781975350321 (v. 10 ; trade paperback) | ISBN 9781975350345 (v. 11 ; trade paperback)
Subjects: GSAFD: Science fiction. | Fantasy fiction.
Classification: LCC PL876.A23 D4813 2021 | DDC 895.63/6—dc23
LC record available at https://lccn.loc.gov/2020054696

ISBNs: 978-1-9753-5034-5 (paperback)
         978-1-9753-5035-2 (ebook)

10 9 8 7 6 5 4 3 2 1

LSC-C

Printed in the United States of America

Spirit

A uniquely catastrophic creature existing in a parallel world. Cause of occurrence and reason for existence unknown. Creates a spacequake and inflicts serious damage on her surroundings whenever she appears in this world. A very powerful fighter.

Strategy No. 1

Annihilate with force. This approach is very difficult, since the Spirit is extremely powerful, as noted above.

Strategy No. 2

...Date her and make her all weak in the knees.

Devil Tobiichi

Spirit No. 1i
Astral Dress—Devil Type
Weapon—Crown Type [Satan]

Chapter 6
Struggling

"Umm, are we about done here?" a timid voice said, and Shido Itsuka jumped.

He had apparently spaced out for a second. He looked in the direction of the voice and found a small woman in glasses—the teacher Tamae Okamine, nicknamed Tama—holding a notebook open toward him and looking troubled. She seemed rooted to the spot by the intensity of Shido's gaze.

"O-oh, yeah. Thank…you," he said with a bow.

It was no wonder, however, that her day planner had stopped him in his tracks like that. The date written on the page she presented to him was five years earlier than his own time. He swallowed hard and then looked around once more.

The familiar city feeling slightly off, waking up in an entirely different season, a Tama who thought he was a stranger—everything corroborated the impossible information noted in her day planner.

"Well then, I'll just be on my way…?" Tama said, cocking her head slightly to one side.

Lost in thought, brow furrowed, Shido abruptly gasped and opened his eyes wide. "Oh. Right. I'm sorry. Thank you."

She craned her neck curiously as she left, and after watching her go, he leaned back against the wall.

"Five years ago? This can't be real," he groaned as he pressed a hand to his forehead. Common sense dictated that this was preposterous and absurd, but that clashed with the multiple pieces of evidence he had already seen.

He still couldn't believe it. Time was irreversible and inviolable. There was no going back to a time that had passed. Anyone coming up through the compulsory education system learned this basic fact while they were still in elementary school.

Unfortunately, Shido couldn't reject the idea out of hand anymore.

A possible explanation suddenly popped into his head. Right before he'd found himself in this predicament, he'd encountered a girl. A very particular girl.

"Ku...rumi." He murmured her name, swallowing to wet his dry throat, and a clear vision of her rose in the back of his mind. The jet-black hair tied up in asymmetrical bundles, pale skin covered by a crimson-and-black dress. And the face of a clock engraved in her left eye.

Kurumi. Kurumi Tokisaki. An unsealed Spirit, considered to be the worst of all of them. Her Angel was Zafkiel, and it had the ability to manipulate time. Each and every one of the numbers on the face of the clock-shaped Angel possessed a different power. When the shadows that spilled out from the clockface were loaded into a gun and fired as bullets, the Angel would speed up the progress of time for the target, stop time entirely, or change their timeline in some other unexpected way.

And seconds before he'd awakened in this world, Kurumi had shot him twice. He swallowed hard as he ran a hand over his forehead to find it free of any injury.

A Spirit who existed beyond reason and her Angel. Given her power, this—

"*Kee-hee-hee! Hee-hee!*"

"...?!"

Quiet laughter broke into his racing thoughts.

"Wh-who's there?!" He whirled his head around.

"*Oh, dear me! How heartbreaking. Have you forgotten me already?*"

"No way..." He gasped at this voice, the tone of it. "Kurumi?!"

"*Yes, indeed. Heh-heh-heh. I am so very glad you recognize me,*" the owner of the voice—Kurumi—continued.

It was a curious feeling. He couldn't see her anywhere, and yet he could hear her voice loud and clear, like an invisible someone was whispering in his ear, or a tiny elf had taken up residence inside his head.

He hurriedly glanced to either side. But he couldn't spot any avatars nearby.

Perhaps finding this amusing, Kurumi giggled. "*Hee-hee-hee. Looking around for me is pointless. After all, I'm in a different time from you, Shido.*"

"Wha…?!" He gasped at this confident declaration.

This *was* the possible explanation that had been lurking in the corners of his mind, but when she confirmed it, his heart nearly stopped beating. Shido felt a terrible anxiety seeping into his bones as he grew more and more confident that he had accidentally wandered into an absolute impossibility.

He worked to get his breathing back under control before saying to Kurumi (wherever she might have been), "I *knew* it. So this is Tengu… five years ago?"

"*Oh, goodness me!*" She sounded surprised. "*So you already figured out when it is? Hee-hee-hee! I suppose I should've expected nothing less of you, Shido.*"

"I just got lucky," he said, furrowing his brow. "But you're gonna explain, right?"

"*Yes,*" she confirmed. "*As you have so cleverly surmised, I took the liberty of sending you to the city of Tengu five years in the past. With the power of Zafkiel's final bullet, Yud Bet.*"

"Yud Bet…" He guessed that this was probably one of Zafkiel's abilities. He'd known from the start that the Angel was extremely powerful, but he never dreamed it could do anything like this.

"*It is also Zafkiel's power that allows me to speak with you now,*" she continued. "*Tet, the ninth bullet. It connects my mind with that of a person on a different time axis. However, since the bullet is fairly limited in its application, I'm not particularly accustomed to using it. It took some effort to establish the connection.*"

"It connects…your mind?" He stared in disbelief into the empty air.

"*Yes. Naturally, that includes conversing in this manner, but I can also sense what you see and hear.*"

"I kinda…don't love that." Shido looked down and opened and closed his hands. Would this sight be transmitted to Kurumi, too? He somehow felt like a remote-controlled robot.

"*Hee-hee-hee!*" she giggled. "*That is why I would recommend that you refrain from any activities you wouldn't be comfortable doing in front of an audience. Although I personally have no objections to such things.*"

"I'm not gonna—!" he shouted reflexively.

A woman who happened to be walking down the road passed him at a brisk pace, like she wanted to put a lot of distance between herself and this obviously suspicious person.

"A-anyway. Send me back to my own time right now!" he pleaded, fists clenched. "I don't have *time* for this! While I'm stuck in the past, Tohka and the others are—!"

Yes. He had to return to his own timeline as soon as possible. His own Tengu City was currently facing a massive, unprecedented catastrophe. An inverted Origami had appeared out of nowhere and started shooting endless destructive beams from the sky that were absolutely devastating the city. Tohka, the Yamai sisters, and Miku were desperately trying to stop her rampage while Yoshino and Natsumi did everything they could to save the countless bystanders on the ground. Not to mention that *Fraxinus* had been shot down by Origami when the ship flew in close to rescue Shido, and he still had no idea if Kotori and her crew were all right. And despite being the only person who could lock away a Spirit's powers, Shido had vanished from the scene. He could only, and all too easily, picture the nightmare unfolding in his own world.

"*Well, I suppose so,*" Kurumi agreed. "*It's quite the spectacle over here. Scorched earth as far as the eye can see. I expect that even hell itself pales in comparison.*"

"…! That's exactly why you have to bring me back!" he cried.

But she only sighed in exasperation, as if to signal that she was aware of the urgency of the situation. *"Are you quite sure about that? You wish to return to your original time without accomplishing anything? After I was kind enough to send you back to the past with Yud Bet, Zafkiel's most secret of secrets?"*

"…?! What are you talking about?" Shido half groaned, failing to understand what she was getting at.

"I mean exactly what I said," she noted, simply. *"If you wish to resolve this doomsday scenario, then you must do something about the Origami in this Tengu of five years ago."*

"Origami…?" He frowned. "H-hang on a second. I don't get it. I mean, yeah, Origami's here, too, but it's the fifth-grade her from five years ago, right? What exactly—?"

"No, that is where you are incorrect," she interrupted. *"The Origami you need to see is the one who has undergone the Spirit transformation. She should have returned to that time with my Yud Bet."*

"What?!" he shrieked reflexively. "Origami's…here?!"

"Yes. Well, I added a touch of extra time when I sent you off, so she won't have appeared yet. But she should arrive before too long."

"But how…?" he started to say. "Why would Origami…?"

"To avenge her parents," Kurumi explained dispassionately. *"Or, to be more precise, to strike down her enemy before there's any loss to avenge."*

"…!!" Shido felt his heart constrict in his chest, and the disjointed pieces of information scattered in his brain converged into one cohesive story—Origami's parents killed by a Spirit five years earlier, her newfound power that transcended human experience, and Kurumi's Yud Bet.

"Origami," he half whispered as he recalled the other Spirit who had been at the scene of the fire five years earlier. "She came back to defeat Phantom? But then why did she invert after she returned to our time? What happened here in *this* time?!"

"Indeed," Kurumi agreed. *"Whatever occurred in that time is a mystery to me as well. Which is why I shot you with Yud Bet. Your job is to investigate and undo it."*

"Everything's starting to make sense." Shido pressed a hand to his chest as if to keep his pounding heart from tearing itself out of his body.

Find Origami and figure out what she was doing five years earlier, pinpoint the cause of the inversion, and fix this. If Kurumi was telling the truth, then this probably was the only way.

But there was still one thing he didn't understand. He did his best to glare at the girl he couldn't see as he moved his lips. "Kurumi. If all this is true, then why would you do this for me? And not just for me. You sent Origami back because she asked you to, right?"

Yes. This was the part that didn't click for him. Kurumi was a notably foreign element, even among the Spirits, who were already far separated from the rational. She had helped him before, but only because doing so was in line with her own interests. He couldn't believe that *this* girl, of all the Spirits, would use her Angel for the benefit of someone else.

She was silent for a moment before replying. *"It's not necessarily the case that...this doesn't benefit me, hmm? I don't often get the opportunity to test out Yud Bet with another's Spirit power. But...I suppose."* She stopped and sighed. *"If I were absolutely forced to give a reason, it's because I want proof."*

"Proof?" He frowned. "Of what exactly?"

"That a person can change history."

He felt like her tone was somehow different from her usual tongue-in-cheek style, and he swallowed hard unconsciously. "Change history..."

"Yes. Please do show me this is possible," she demanded. *"Please make it as though this hopeless destruction, this irremediable tragedy, never happened."*

"I... Can I *do* that? I heard history has the power to correct itself," Shido said, looking troubled. He wasn't particularly well-versed in science fiction, but he'd watched a certain time-travel movie and learned about this particular theory. Basically, even if you did use a time machine to go back into the past and do something significant enough to change history, an event similar to the one you prevented would occur to compensate for the change, maintaining the course of history.

But. Kurumi cackled at this. *"You do say the* strangest *things, don't you, Shido!"*

He heard a bewitching sigh inside his brain. If she had actually been there in person, she would no doubt have nudged his chin up provocatively.

"Who exactly espoused this theory to you? Did this scholar actually cross time to prove their hypothesis?"

"I—I mean…," he stammered.

"No matter how great and vast the world might be, the only one who can interfere with inviolable time is me, Kurumi Tokisaki," she said coolly. It sounded almost like she was talking more to herself than to Shido. *"My Zafkiel is the only way. Please pay no mind to the foolish ramblings of big-headed scholars and authors. What you, Shido, see with those eyes of yours is the only truth."*

"Kurumi…?" he asked tentatively.

"We've spent too long chatting," she replied, regaining her usual cheeky tone. *"Although I did give you a head start when I shot you with Yud Bet, you can't simply stand there forever. Shall we begin?"*

Shido gritted his teeth and nodded. There were a million things he still didn't understand. But she was right about one thing, at least— this was the only way to stop Origami's inversion and save the city from descending into pure chaos.

"Yeah… Let's go, Kurumi." He raised his head and turned around.

Origami's objective was to defeat the Spirit that had killed her parents. And that Spirit had most likely been Phantom. In which case, she would appear in Tengu's Nanko district, the site of the great fire.

He clenched a hand into a fist, preparing himself to start running in that direction. He didn't know what time it was exactly, but the sun was already angling downward. The midsummer sun, however, knew nothing of weakness and beat down on him mercilessly with searing heat. With every move he made, sweat poured from his body, and his stamina plummeted.

But he didn't stop. He was partly spurred on by the fact that he didn't know how long he'd be able to stay here like this. But the biggest factor pushing him forward was the feeling that he couldn't sit back quietly when Tohka and the other Spirits were fighting so hard in his own era.

Before too long, he arrived at a familiar place.

"Nanko…" He panted between ragged breaths, gradually slackening his pace.

Yes. Spreading out before him was the district of Nanko before the fire had visited it. A strange sensation overcame him. He was shaken with something akin to nostalgia or homesickness by the sight of this city he'd once lived in.

"Ah…" His feet automatically stopped abruptly.

"What is the matter, Shido?" Kurumi asked dubiously. But he couldn't respond.

His attention was focused on a house. A two-story building with a distinctive dark red roof. It was absent of any features that would particularly draw the eye, but the moment he caught sight of it, he found himself rooted in place, like he'd been shot.

This was the house he'd lived in until five years ago. But his feet hadn't stopped because of the house itself. The moment he saw it, a thought had flitted through his mind.

Five years ago… Shido was currently in the Tengu City from five years in the past. On the day that Origami had lost both of her parents at the hand of a Spirit and sworn in her heart to destroy the Spirits.

But that wasn't the only thing that had happened on that day. At that impossible moment when Origami saw the target of her revenge, the town had been wrapped in flames, in a blaze brought about by his own little sister, Kotori Itsuka.

Kurumi had told him to make contact with the Origami who had also returned to the past, to prevent her inversion from ever happening. But a new possibility occurred to him. What if…he could also make it so Kotori hadn't been turned into a Spirit by Phantom five years ago? If she was in the house right now, maybe he could tell her not to go to the park where she would meet Phantom.

As soon as he had this thought, his feet automatically turned and started moving toward his own house.

His memory was hazy, but he was pretty sure that on that fateful August 3, he had gone into town to buy a birthday present for Kotori. He wouldn't accidentally run into his younger self here. He opened the gate with a familiar hand, crossed the yard, and walked around to the back of the house.

As he did, he caught the "Itsuka" nameplate out of the corner of his eye, which perhaps tipped Kurumi off to what he was doing.

"*Shido,*" she said in a slightly forceful tone. "*I do understand how you must feel, but please, you can't go after Kotori.*"

"I'm going to deal with Origami!" he protested. "I just—"

"*That is not the issue,*" she interjected. "*You can't be unaware of what could happen if Kotori did not become a Spirit five years ago, hmm?*"

"…! Ah—" His eyes flew open.

Dizzied as he was by the possibility that his sister wouldn't have to become a Spirit, his train of thought hadn't even gotten that far. But if Kotori didn't become a Spirit…she wouldn't be discovered by Ratatoskr. And if that didn't happen, Ratatoskr wouldn't find out about Shido's sealing powers, and the Spirit powers of Tohka, Yoshino, Kaguya, Yuzuru, Miku, and Natsumi might never be locked away. Above all, he couldn't let that happen.

Shido gritted his teeth in frustration and shook his head. "Sorry. I lost my cool."

"*Not at all. The possibility of changing the past is both an alluring wine and a poisonous chalice that drives people mad,*" Kurumi said, sounding wise. "*I cannot fault you for that, Shido.*"

A hint of a frown crossed his face. He couldn't help but feel that Kurumi was also giving herself a warning, just like she'd been talking more to herself before.

But when he thought about it, that was only natural. The potential to change the past… Who wouldn't be tempted? He couldn't even begin to imagine how much the possibilities had tortured Kurumi when she held the power to make it all happen.

"Hey, Kurumi? You—," he started to say, and then he heard a voice from the gate.

"Itsukaaaaa! It's Suzumoto from next dooooor!"

"…?!" He jumped at the sudden call.

"Are you here? I'm coming in!"

He heard the sound of the gate opening.

Suzumoto had lived next door to them five years earlier. She often shared the vegetables and other things her family in the country sent to her. Now that he was thinking about it, he remembered how they'd frequently come home to vegetables sitting in front of the back door.

Shido had always considered her deliveries a blessing, but her timing now could not have been worse. He was not the elementary school boy who should have been in the yard but a high schooler five years older. He looked like an intruder, no question about it. If she called the police, the ensuing chaos would cost him precious time.

"I—I gotta do something!" He panicked, looking around for an escape.

Suzumoto's footsteps grew steadily closer. There was nowhere for him to hide. His back was against the wall. And then a thought occurred to him.

"Hmm?" Naoko Suzumoto, the housewife who lived next door to the Itsukas, stepped into the Itsukas' backyard and noticed a child, probably in grade five or six. His face was adorable in a way that made it hard to tell if he was a boy or a girl.

"Shido, you're here!" she said. "Sorry. No one answered when I rang the bell, so I came around back."

"N-no! *I'm* sorry. I guess I didn't hear it." Shido, the Itsukas' oldest, had an awkward smile on his face for some reason.

Naoko tilted her head curiously to one side, and then held the plastic bag in her hand out toward him. "Here. My family in the countryside sent them. I thought I'd share with you all."

"Th-thank you. This is great." He accepted the plastic bag and bowed neatly.

"Oh dear?" She frowned.

"Um," he said. "Is something the matter?"

"No, no. You just seem different today, Shido."

"Huh?! O-oh, I don't really think I am, though."

"No? Hmm. I suppose it's just in my head. Well, that's fine, then. Say hi to your mom for me."

"Okay. Thank you."

Naoko left the Itsukas' yard with Shido's voice at her back.

"Haaah…" Shido let out a huge sigh as he watched Suzumoto walk away.

"Hee-hee-hee!" Kurumi giggled. *"You always think on your feet, hmm, Shido?"*

"I'm just really glad that worked," he replied as he wiped the sweat away. He could feel that the hand he drew across his forehead was smaller than the one in his memory. And it wasn't only his hand. His torso, his feet, and even the clothes on his body were all smaller.

Yes. What popped into Shido's head when he was on the verge of being discovered by his neighbor was the time Natsumi had turned the other Spirits into children with her Angel Haniel.

It would be totally normal for a younger Shido to be here now. More importantly, he had Natsumi's Spirit power locked away inside him. So he decided to try to see if he could make it happen. Unlike Tohka's Sandalphon or Yoshino's Zadkiel, he'd never manifested this Angel before, but he seemed to have managed it pretty well.

"Sorry for the delay. Let's go." He set the plastic bag Suzumoto had given him down in front of the house.

However.

"Hmm?"

"Whatever is the matter?" Kurumi asked.

"Oh, uh. How do I reverse this?" He frowned, while sweat rolled down his cheek. He'd changed quite suddenly, and he didn't know how to undo it.

"Oh my, oh dear. This is quite the pickle. And you really have to go find Origami now."

"Mm. I gotta do something and turn back." Shido lowered his eyes and groaned, and Kurumi giggled inside his head.

Shido, before you turn back, would you be so kind as to stand in front of a mirror?

"Huh?" He furrowed his brow, confused. "Why?"

From where I am, I'm unable to see your currently very adorable little face, she told him.

"You're unbelievable." He sighed and rolled his eyes.

But in that moment, the sky abruptly flashed red, and he turned in that direction with a gasp.

An enormous pillar of flames shot into the sky on the other side of the neat rows of roofs before bouncing back and bathing the area in a wave of sweltering heat.

The whole neighborhood was ablaze in the blink of an eye, with houses and trees all around catching fire. He heard screams in every direction, and the neighbors began to flee.

"Is this…Kotori?!" he cried.

It does seem that way, doesn't it? Kurumi replied.

He gritted his teeth in anger and frustration. Apparently, Kotori had already gone to the park. And been made into the Spirit Efreet by Phantom.

"Ngh!" He started running. Just standing there wasn't doing him any good. His body was still small, but he didn't have the time to figure out how to return to normal. The fact that Kotori had become a Spirit meant that Phantom was there with her—and that Origami would soon arrive in this time to meet the mysterious Spirit.

But between the crowds of people fleeing and houses crumbling in the inferno, the road was clogged, and he couldn't make any real progress.

Digging into his own memories of five years earlier, he decided to take a detour and managed to make it to the park.

"…! There—!"

Shido spotted three people ahead of him. One was the sobbing baby Kotori. The second was the younger Shido lying flat on the ground. And standing there looking down on them was a *something* veiled by static.

"Phantom!" Shido shouted as a beam of light shot down from above, and the figure of Phantom disappeared.

"…!" He felt something like sparks flying inside his head.

Yes. He'd seen this before. Five years earlier, there had indeed been a bolt from the heavens aimed at Phantom. He lifted his face with a gasp, searching for the source of this light.

He managed to spot another figure in the sky. A beautiful girl, wrapped in a stunning white dress and accompanied by what looked like so many feathers. But hatred and rage twisted her face.

"Origami…!" he shouted.

Yes. The one flying in the sky was the Spirit Origami Tobiichi, who had crossed time and space to come here. It was still a mystery to him how she had been turned into a Spirit. But the Origami here and now hadn't inverted yet. Most likely, the incident that would push her to the brink of despair was about to happen.

He also saw Phantom up in the sky with her. The mysterious Spirit had probably dodged Origami's blow and flown up there.

Origami waved a hand, and the feathers floating around her shot beams of light at Phantom.

As if this were the signal, the two Spirits began to race around the sky.

"Shido, please do go after them. You'll lose sight of them at this rate."

"R-right!" Jolted into motion by Kurumi's voice, Shido began to run once more, racing through the burning streets to chase after the Spirits.

Origami fired again and again, relentless in her attack, but Phantom merely continued to dodge. They flew up and down and around, almost as though they were playing tag. He didn't see anything that even resembled a counterattack.

"Origami! Origami! It's me, Shido! Listen to me! You can't do this!" he shouted desperately as he ran, but he got no response.

But that was only natural. Not only was she physically far away, she'd finally found her most hated enemy and had them in her sights. Origami might have been very powerful, but it was no surprise that she was entirely focused on her revenge.

That didn't mean Shido could just give up, though. Furiously chasing after the two, he kept yelling, "Origami! Origamiiii!"

"Origami!"

When he heard someone else cry out her name, Shido stopped in his tracks. "Huh...?"

Wrenching his gaze away from the battle in the sky, he saw a married couple standing not too far from him. They had likely fled their burning home; their clothes were dirty, and he could see scratches on their exposed skin.

For a heartbeat, he wondered why they were calling Origami's name, but then he caught sight of a young girl standing in front of them, and he understood everything.

Hair that came down to her shoulders and the face of a bright, sharp child. Yes, this was...Origami from five years ago.

"Mom! Dad!" she called out, tears springing from her eyes in sheer joy at seeing that her parents were all right.

And then everything in Shido's field of view went white.

"...?!"

A tremendous shock wave ripped through the area, and his small body was easily sent flying.

"Hngh!" He let out a cry of pain as he slammed into a concrete wall.

"Shido, are you all right?" Kurumi asked.

"Y-yeah... More or less. But—" He managed to pull himself up somehow and started scanning for Origami and what he assumed were her parents.

"Wha...?" Any words he might have said died in his throat.

There was a massive crater where the couple had stood, and parts of what had been people a mere instant earlier were scattered all around. This gruesome sight would have caused most people to automatically empty the contents of their stomachs. But Shido could only stare, rooted to the spot.

Because five years ago, he'd seen Origami witness this tragedy from close up.

"Ah... Ah... Aaaaaaah!" Screaming hoarsely, Origami crawled along the ground, desperately trying to cling to what had once been her parents. As her teeth chattered, she lifted her face to glare at the source of the light that had poured from the sky.

"An...angel," she murmured, still looking up.

Shido followed suit and raised his own face to the heavens. "...! It...can't be...," he muttered to himself. His voice shook, and a chill hit him that made him feel like insects were crawling all over him.

Yes. There. In the sky, he saw the Spirit Origami wrapped in her snowy-white Astral Dress. From here, he couldn't make out the face of the Spirit who had fired the light pillar. The eyes of the younger Origami would have been able to perceive the older girl's silhouette only from far above. It was understandable that someone who knew nothing of the Spirits would describe the figure as an angel.

"Y...ou..." As Origami crumpled to the ground, her childish eyes were filled with pure rage. She howled, "You won't get away with this! I'll kill you... I will kill you! And that's a promise!"

There was no way her voice could have reached that far up, but the Origami in the spotless white Astral Dress shuddered and twisted as the girl spat these words at her. To the casual observer, it might have looked as though she were laughing.

But Shido knew painfully well that there was no way that could be true.

"How...can this be happening?!"

Mere seconds passed. But in those brief moments, everything happened, and everything ended. At last, Shido understood.

Origami had returned to the moment her parents were killed five years earlier and tried to prevent that tragedy. But now she knew. She knew the true identity of the person who'd killed her mother and father.

"*Well, now I see,*" Kurumi said inside his head, looking out at the world through Shido's eyes. "*I did think something quite significant must have happened to transform someone such as Origami into that, but...*"

The Spirit hanging in the sky disappeared as if melting into the air itself.

"...?!" Shido gasped. "She disappeared?"

"*Most likely, Yud Bet's effect ended,*" Kurumi replied. "*I suppose she's returned to her own time.*"

"...! But then...!" he cried in alarm. His objective—and the reason

Kurumi had sent him to the world of five years ago—was to investigate the cause of Origami's inversion and resolve it. And they had certainly discovered the cause. But at the same time, the Spirit in question was out of reach now. They wouldn't be able to change history like this.

"Wh-what exactly are we supposed to—?" At a total loss, Shido gasped and cut himself off.

The reason was simple. Chunks of burning building were about to fall directly on top of where the young Origami had sunk down to the ground.

"Origami!" he cried, and before the word was fully out of his mouth, he was leaping toward her. He used this momentum to grab hold of Origami and roll the two of them out of harm's way.

In the next instant, fiery debris struck the ground, raising a huge cloud of dust and dancing sparks.

"Hngh!" Shido coughed as he took Origami's hand and started running down the red road. It was too dangerous to stay here any longer.

He stopped after he'd whisked them away to a place where the flickering flames didn't reach, where Origami immediately dropped to her knees.

"Haaah! Haaah! You okay, Origami?" he said, before realizing his own error. He'd acted on instinct, but this Origami wouldn't know who he was. It was maybe not great that he had shouted her name.

But this fear of his ended up unfounded.

Origami seemed to not even register this total stranger calling her by name. She simply shook helplessly and looked up at the sky with empty eyes.

No. The word *empty* was not quite right. Rage, hatred, loss, grief— every sort of negative human emotion mingled together in her eyes.

"Dad… Mom…" Those terribly quiet words fell from her dry, cracked lips.

"…!" Shido unconsciously grimaced at her obvious pain.

"I—I…," she stammered.

"Origami!" He didn't know what to do. He didn't know what to say. But he couldn't leave her like this. Barely thinking about it, he wrapped his trembling arms around her. Tightly, very tightly, like he wanted to cut off the wild waves of emotion roiling inside him.

"...Y...ou..." Origami's voice was small, like she had only just noticed Shido's presence.

"It's okay! You're okay!" he half groaned, half howled, still holding her. He knew these words were hollow and irresponsible, at best. Even so, he had to say them.

The small girl, so tiny that Shido could completely wrap her up with his similarly small arms, faced a world that was too inhumane, too ruthless. The hardship that lay ahead and the truth she would inevitably arrive at were so cruel that he felt compelled to cry out and rail against this fate.

"Origami," he said. "I know...you'll figure it out one day...the truth about...everything! But don't forget...! You're not alone!"

"What are you...?" she replied, looking perplexed. Who could blame her? But Shido couldn't stop himself.

"I'll take on all your sadness! Your anger! When you're lost, you can lean on me! When you just can't take it anymore, you can use me! Hit me with whatever! So! So...!" He squeezed her even more tightly. "Just... Just don't give in to despair!"

"...!" Origami gaped at him, and soon, her entire body was shaking. "Ah. Unh. Ah... Unnnh. Waaaah! Aaaaah!" She grabbed hold of his shirt, buried her face in his chest, and began to let out strangled sobs.

Maybe his appearance had relieved her of whatever tension had been holding her upright, or perhaps the grief of losing her parents was hitting her at last. He couldn't tell which it was, but he finally saw a glimpse of the emotion he expected from such a young girl.

"D-Dad... Mom!" she wailed.

"Origami..." He stroked her back with a trembling hand as she sobbed and sobbed.

After a while, Origami released Shido's shirt and got to her feet. "Th-thank you...," she said in a quiet voice. After wiping her tears away with her sleeve, she focused her bloodshot eyes on him. "So... who are you anyway?"

"Oh! Uh. Umm." This was an extremely natural question, but when she asked it so suddenly, Shido had no idea how to respond. He couldn't really make up some weird cover story. He met her eyes, and without thinking much about his answer, he blurted, "I'm Shido Itsuka. I live around here."

"Shido...Itsuka," Origami murmured, chewing on his name before whirling around, like she was trying to hide the expression on her face. "... Did you mean what you said?"

"Huh?" He frowned, uncomprehending.

"Will you take on everything for me?"

"O-oh! Yeah, I meant that." He nodded firmly. Although the words had come out of him on impulse, he was ready to stand by what he said.

"You did? Okay," she continued, still not looking at his face. "Then I'll give you my tears. I'll give you my smile. Please take everything fun, happy, and nice."

"Huh?" Shido's eyes grew wide in surprise.

"This is the last time I'll cry. It's also the last time I'll smile," she said as she turned back toward him.

When Shido saw the smile on her tearstained face, he didn't know what to say.

Origami turned her face away again. "But this anger is mine. This ugly thing is all mine. I'll kill that...angel. No matter how long it takes. No matter what I have to do."

"..."

Angel. The word made his fingers tremble. But he couldn't tell her that this Spirit was the future her. He couldn't say something like that to this painfully small girl.

"So please keep these things for me until then. Until I...kill the angel," Origami said, her back still turned.

"Ori...gami..." Shido could only say her name in a daze.

The too-young spirit of vengeance ran off, leaving him all alone.

◇

"…"

In the descending darkness, Kurumi let out a weary sigh. "I see what happened now…"

She was peering into two different worlds at the same time, through a mind that also shared Shido's senses. If she opened her eyes, she beheld a city on the verge of total destruction, enduring the rain of jet-black beams pouring from the inverted Origami in the sky; if she closed them, she saw the back of an Origami five years younger, swearing revenge on the Spirit as she left.

Now Kurumi knew everything, just like Shido. She understood the reason why Origami had inverted after returning to this time period.

"Ironic, isn't it?" She lifted her face to study the girl floating in the obsidian sky. None of the Origami that Kurumi knew remained in this Spirit far overhead.

Clad in a funereal jet-black Astral Dress, the Spirit was curled up like a fetus buoyed by amniotic fluid, drifting through the sky. Countless feathers of various sizes hung around her in a circle, and her destructive impulses rained down on the earth below.

"What to do, what to do?" Kurumi murmured, stroking her chin. It was all fine and good to have sent Shido back in time, but all they'd managed to do was pinpoint the cause of Origami's inversion. If they didn't figure something out…

"Oh dear?" She arched an eyebrow abruptly and looked back. Quiet footsteps approached from behind. "And who might you be? Do you have some business with me?" she said, to challenge the mysterious visitor.

A heartbeat later, her guest responded by taking another step forward.

"…! You—" Her eyes flew open in surprise.

"I…" After watching Origami walk away, Shido dropped to his knees, overwhelmed by helplessness. In the end, he hadn't been able to change a single thing.

But strangely, the ground began to pull away from him despite the fact that he was kneeling in place.

"Huh?"

For a second, he thought his body was moving against his will, but that wasn't it. He looked down at himself and saw that his body was quickly returning to its original size. Perhaps the effect of the Spirit power he'd used had run out, or some set time limit had been reached. Or maybe there was another reason. He didn't know exactly why, but it was clear that Natsumi's spell had ended.

"I don't like this at all." Kurumi's voice in his head sounded peeved.

"Sorry," he said. "I know you used Yud Bet and everything, but—"

"That is not what I am talking about." Kurumi continued with a sigh. *"The person who killed Origami's parents was Origami herself? True, that might be enough to explain her despair. However...this obviously could not have happened without my Zafkiel."*

He heard the distinct sound of gnashing teeth, something the usually composed Kurumi never did.

"Shido. Allow me to ask you a question. When did you first meet Origami?"

"Huh? Uh." He paused briefly. "We got shuffled into new classes at the start of grade eleven, so then, I guess."

"And at that time, perhaps Origami seemed to know you already, although you assumed that it was your first meeting?"

Shido thought back. It was true that Origami had known his name then. And then it hit him. "Oh."

Of course Origami had already known him. She had met him five years earlier.

"This is absolutely no fun at all." Kurumi sounded even more displeased. *"How unpleasant. How very...disagreeable."*

"Kurumi?" he said hesitantly.

"The reason for Origami's hatred of the Spirits... Your meeting with Origami...," Kurumi said, as if reciting a monologue. *"My power is the primary element. If I hadn't sent Origami and then you back in time, the world as we know it would not exist..."*

Maybe she was right. Without the Spirit Kurumi and the Angel Zafkiel, then the world Shido lived in would have probably become something else entirely.

"O-okay, but come on," he protested. "It's not like you used Zafkiel to do this on purpose, right, Kurumi?"

"*No, of course not,*" she snapped. "*But the act of attempting to change history itself is one of the central building blocks of this history, this world. You might think you are pushing desperately, but in the end, you're doing nothing more than dancing in the palm of the world. What an outrageously infuriating fact.*"

"…!" Shido unconsciously gasped at the hard edge in her voice. But at the same time, a thought popped into his head. He opened his mouth. "Kurumi… Is there something you want to do over, too?"

She was silent for a moment before reverting to her usual playful tone. "*My, my. Now that we're talking about it, I might enjoy redoing my first meeting with you, Shido. Hee-hee-hee! With my current power, I could most certainly eat the old you, hmm?*"

"…" He clamped his mouth shut. But not out of fear at her ominous statement. He dropped the subject because he guessed that she was trying to deflect. He wasn't the sort to force someone to talk when they obviously didn't want to. And he had a million other things that required his attention at the moment.

"Either way, it's all over," he said, clenching his fists in frustration.

Now that Origami had returned to their original world, he couldn't stop her inversion. And now that the younger Origami had witnessed her parents being killed, he couldn't erase the desire for vengeance from her heart. To borrow Kurumi's words, he was merely dancing in the palm of the world's hand. He didn't know how much longer Yud Bet would last, but sooner or later, he would also return to his original world, where the inverted Origami was on a rampage.

"I…suppose so," Kurumi responded. "*Indeed, it's exactly as you say. You were unable to stop Origami, Shido. You weren't able to change anything. It would seem that this world's future is set in stone.*"

"Kurumi...?" He furrowed his brow. Something about the way she put this felt slightly off to him.

Likely sensing his unspoken question, she giggled. *"At any rate, it does appear that the matter is settled. Or so I was told just now."*

"Told?" His frown grew even deeper. "By whom, exactly?"

"By you in half an hour or so."

"Huh?" Shido's eyes widened like saucers. "What's that supposed to...?"

"It means exactly what I said," she replied neatly. *"A half an hour or so from now, after accomplishing nothing, the me of the world you return to uses Yud Bet and sends the future Shido to me. Well, you returned to your original time after about a minute, perhaps to conserve Spirit power, so we weren't really able to talk too much, though."*

"...?! A Kurumi further in the future?!" Shido felt his jaw actually drop. But when he thought about it, this wasn't an impossible scenario. After all, he and Origami had already traveled five years into the past, thanks to Kurumi's power. Given that there was also a Kurumi in the future, there was no reason she couldn't use that same power to send a future someone to the present.

However. This brought up an important question for Shido. "Why would...future me go to the trouble of traveling through time?" he asked slowly.

Yes. The whole thing strained credulity. Yud Bet was supposed to be Kurumi's trump card. It was hard to imagine she would use her precious time just to communicate a bleak future to herself.

"Yes," the Kurumi in his head said. *"It appears that after the effects of Yud Bet wore off, you returned to your own world and despaired over how you failed to stop Origami. But you apparently reached a certain conclusion after that."*

"A certain...conclusion?" he replied dubiously.

"Yes." He could almost hear her nodding. *"But since you had returned to your original world, you were no longer able to carry it out, see?"*

"...! Oh. Yeah, I do."

So future Shido asked future Kurumi to send him back in time half an hour so he could tell the past Kurumi what to do—since at this point in time, Shido was still five years in the past. In order to rewrite history and shatter the future, he'd entrusted his hope to his past self.

Shido felt a flame roar to life once more, setting his stilled heart ablaze. "Kurumi…!"

"*It does appear that all is not yet lost, hmm? We'll do it, Shido,*" she declared stridently. "*Let us smash this shithole of a world.*"

Shido unconsciously gasped at this very un-Kurumi-like expression, and then the corners of his lips turned up. "Yeah. I'll do whatever it takes. To save everyone—to save Origami."

"*Hee-hee-hee!*" Kurumi laughed merrily inside his head. She'd no doubt picked up on his excitement. "*I do love that burgeoning spirit of yours.*"

"So then…how do we do this smashing?" he asked.

"*Now that I think about it, it's actually quite obvious,*" she replied. "*But the method is perhaps not one you could see clearly in your panic and despair.*"

"Hngh…" Shido felt a trickle of sweat running down his cheek. "A-anyway… We're running out of time. Let's get a move on."

"*Yes, yes, you're absolutely right. Time is far more precious than money,*" she said, a teasing note in her voice. "*The biggest reason why you were unable to stop Origami, Shido, simply comes down to the fact that you didn't know what was going to happen.*"

"Yeah. I guess that was the real issue," he agreed, screwing up his face in a pained expression.

A second after he'd spotted Origami arriving from their original world, the battle with Phantom had started, and before he could basically even take a breath, it was all over. If he'd known the particulars in advance, there might have been a card he could have played.

Kurumi let out a somehow weary sigh. "*To be honest, I don't particularly care for the idea… But we do in fact have options still.*"

"Huh?" He frowned. "L-like what?"

"*The logic of it is simple,*" she told him. "*We do it over one more time.*"

"Uh…?" He let out a baffled cry. "W-well, yeah, I guess. You mean using Yud Bet once I'm back in our original timeline and sending me back again, right?"

"*That isn't very practical,*" she averred. "*A relatively large amount of the Spirit power stored in your body would be consumed when I fire Yud Bet. It may not be impossible, but I'm not pleased at the idea of using up so much of what I plan to eat later.*"

"You know, you—," he started to say and then stopped. "Wait, you mean you used the Spirit power inside me for this trip in time, too?"

"*Hee-hee-hee! Well, yes, of course. I may have done this on a bit of a whim, but I'm not so kind as to use my own Spirit power on your behalf, you know?*" she said, as if daring him to take issue with it. And he had plenty of things he wanted to say, but he decided to hold his tongue for the time being. Kurumi continued. "*But if you travel from your current point in time, a redo should be possible with just a little push.*"

"…!" He gasped. "Oh! O-of course!"

Kurumi was exactly right.

"*Yud Bet layering,*" she said. "*Yes, indeed, it is an interesting thought. Although naturally, if it's not done while the first bullet is still in effect, I believe you will be forcibly returned to your own time, Shido.*"

"Th-then we have to hurry!" he cried. "Quick! Kurumi, shoot me with Yud Bet!"

She sighed, sounding exasperated. "*At the moment, I am merely borrowing your senses, Shido. I cannot effect any change in the past. The mere idea that Zafkiel's bullets could reach you there!*"

"S-so then, what am I supposed to do?!" Shido couldn't help but shout, and Kurumi sighed again, which sounded like she'd breathed right in his ear.

"*There is one way, isn't there?*"

He furrowed his brow. "Huh…?"

A few minutes later, Shido was climbing the emergency stairs of a building not too far from the scene of the fire.

"Haaah… Haaah…" He'd been doing nothing but running, and his body had been screaming in agony for a while now. And the heat of the summer, mixed with the intensity of the blaze, mercilessly chipped away at his stamina.

But he couldn't sit around and whine about it. He could only stay in this moment in time for a little longer. He trudged up the emergency stairs, feet clanging loudly on each step.

Before too long, he came out onto the roof and looked around, panting. "Is this...the right place?"

"*Yes, I believe there's probably no mistake,*" Kurumi replied vaguely.

"What do you mean 'probably'...?" He rolled his eyes. Getting his breathing under control, he stepped away from the door and moved toward a blind spot near the edge of the roof.

The building looked down over the residential area, and he could clearly see the Nanko district still burning brightly. The sirens of fire trucks and ambulances filled the air, making the evening town boil with activity.

"..." He shifted his gaze, as if trying to avert his eyes from the appalling scene, and scanned the roof once more to make sure he hadn't overlooked anything.

But there was nothing.

"Hey, there's no one here," he said. "Maybe you got it wrong?"

"*How very strange. That shouldn't—,*" Kurumi started to say, and Shido abruptly felt a chill run up his spine. He was frozen in place.

"Ah!" He swallowed hard. His instincts screamed that someone was behind him.

"Oh dear, oh my." The voice sounded amused.

He knew this voice.

"..." He slowly raised his hands as he turned, so as not to entice the apex predator standing at his back.

"Well, well. I rarely have visitors here," Kurumi said, a bewitching smile spreading across her face.

Chapter 7
Phantom

"You…? From five years ago?!" Shido cried in surprise a few minutes after he reached the roof of the building.

"*Yes,*" Kurumi affirmed. "*Just as I mentioned to you earlier, the only one who can interfere with time in this world is me. And five years ago, there was exactly one person who possessed Zafkiel—me.*"

"But I have only a limited amount of time here, right? If I go looking for her now—"

"*There is no need for concern.*" She cut him off. "*I'm quite certain that I was nearby five years ago.*"

"Nearby…?" He started to frown at the too-good-to-be-true coincidence, and then opened his eyes wide in surprise. "Oh! You're not maybe saying that…you also met *me* five years ago…are you?"

"*No. If my recollection serves, nothing of the sort happened. The reason I was so nearby was because I came to see the flames that broke out so suddenly.*"

"You came to see the flames?"

"*Isn't it a distinct possibility that a disaster of this scale might just happen to involve a Spirit?*" she mused.

"…" Shido broke out in a sweat. If he hadn't sealed Kotori's powers, maybe Kurumi would have discovered them both and made a meal of that power.

Perhaps picking up on something from his silence, Kurumi giggled. *"You're terrible. I'm not as faithless as you fear."*

"Y-yeah," he replied vaguely and cleared his throat, as if pulling himself together again.

"I was nearby five years ago." She continued. *"However, I did not meet you, I will guarantee that. But—no, actually because of that, there's significance in this act."*

"Meaning what?" he asked.

"Please think about it. If you are able to meet me…would that not count as changing history, however slight the change?"

"I guess…it might."

"At any rate, you should hurry," she urged. *"As I mentioned earlier, you haven't much wiggle room."*

"Yeah, I know," he said, clenching his hands into fists. "So then tell me, Kurumi. Where do I go?"

And now here he was.

"…"

Breathing deeply to try to calm his heart that was pounding like an alarm clock, he stared at the lone girl standing on the roof of the building.

It was Kurumi, looking exactly the same as she did in his memory. Actually, to be more precise, what was the same was her age; she was dressed a little differently. A monotone blouse and a lacy skirt with ruffles. And rather than being tied up, her hair was held in place by a hair band with a rose. Even more distinctive was her face. She wore a medical eye patch over her left eye, as if to hide the clockface he knew would be there.

Shido furrowed his brow slightly at this. And then he said, so quietly that basically only the Kurumi in his head could hear him, "Kurumi? Why are you wearing an eye patch?"

"Please pay that no mind."

"Are you maybe hurt?"

"*Please pay that no mind.*"

"But..."

"*Please. Pay. That. No. Mind,*" she said rather forcefully, and he fell silent.

The past Kurumi standing before him tilted her head adorably to one side in a playful gesture. "Oh my, oh dear, oh goodness. Whatever are you mumbling about? What business have you in a place like this?"

Her tone was relaxed and amicable. But there wasn't even a hint of anything resembling carelessness. Although her face was composed in a smile, her eyes were quietly and thoroughly observing Shido's appearance and actions.

But he was running out of time. He steeled himself as he opened his mouth. "Kurumi!" he cried. "I need a favor!"

"Oh my?" She raised a curious eyebrow. "To think that you know my name... Who exactly are you?" She raised her right hand as she spoke. An antique pistol leaped up from the shadows pooling at her feet and tucked itself neatly into her hand. She turned the barrel of the gun on him, and Shido was quick to wave his hands.

"H-hang on a second! I'm not here to—!" A bullet ripped into the ground at his feet. "Gah!"

"Please do not move without my express permission. I have several questions. I'm afraid I make no guarantees for your life in the event that you do not respond correctly." She looked ready to shoot him right in the heart if he didn't answer her questions.

He raised his hands. "I-I'm Shido Itsuka. I come from five years in the future! Using Kurumi's—your power!"

"What did you say?" The look on her face changed instantly. "If you are making a joke, then know that you're playing with more than fire."

"Like I'd be standing here as a joke!" he cried. "Please, you have to listen to me!"

"..." Kurumi narrowed her eyes, as though measuring his sincerity.

"*Oh goodness...,*" an exasperated voice said inside his head. "*The old me is rather cautious, hmm? I would prefer this didn't go on too long. Shido, please try to touch that me somehow.*"

"Touch...?" He groaned. "You're asking for the impossible."

"Did you say something?" Kurumi furrowed her brow dubiously, the barrel of her gun still on him. This was only natural. From her perspective, it could have only looked like he was having a whole conversation with himself.

He reached out toward her, steeling himself for her to fire at him again. "Please. Could you take my hand? You can keep the gun on me."

"You do realize I am not such a babe as to blithely obey when a total stranger says something like that to me, yes?" she snapped.

"*Kurumi says she wants to talk to you,*" he replied.

"...!" Her eyebrow shot up. Her abilities were what allowed him to share his senses with the Kurumi of his own time, after all. This Kurumi must have also had an inkling of this.

"Hmph. Is that so?" Without letting her guard down, Kurumi glared at him as she walked over and touched his hand.

"...!" She shuddered as though a weak electrical current was running through her body.

"*It's been a while,*" Kurumi said. "*I suppose that's the best way to phrase it. Hello, me.*"

"I see... This is indeed...my voice. What exactly has happened in the world five years from now?" The Kurumi from the past could apparently also hear the voice of future Kurumi echoing in Shido's head. And this was indeed much more persuasive than anything he could have done.

The Kurumi from his timeline briefly explained the situation. How they had failed to change history. And how they wanted to get this Kurumi's help to try one last do-over.

"Are you saying that I should shoot this person with Yud Bet?" Kurumi asked. "Me?"

"*Yes. That's exactly what I'm saying. I wonder if you would be so kind, me?*"

The Kurumi of five years earlier fell briefly silent before letting out a short sigh. "I suppose I could. Although I don't have much to offer, I would be willing to be of service."

"R-really?!" Shido cried.

"Yes. But I'll be collecting the necessary Spirit power from you."
Kurumi let go of his hand and stepped back, heels clacking. And then
she stepped down hard with both feet as she brandished her left hand
high in the air. "Now, now, come to me, Zafkiel. Your time has come."

A massive clockface appeared from the shadows—Kurumi's Angel
Zafkiel, which controlled time and had sent Shido to this era.

Meanwhile, the shadow lurking at her feet swelled, expanding
in area and tangling itself beneath his feet. In the next moment, an
incredible weariness overcame him.

"Hngh..."

He recognized this sensation. It was the same feeling as when he'd
been caught by Kurumi immediately before being sent to this time
from his original world.

"Zafkiel. Yud Bet." Kurumi held the gun in her hand directly above
her head. A dense shadow oozed from the XII on Zafkiel's clockface
and poured into the barrel. "Now. I'll just go ahead, then."

She turned the barrel of the gun on him in a leisurely motion. He
knew that being shot by Yud Bet wasn't painful, but he still shrank
back reflexively.

"Shido... That's your name, yes?" she said. "I wish you success."

He stared at her for a second. "Uh, thanks. And Kurumi?"

"Hmm? What is it?"

"I think that eye patch suits you."

"...!"

"Oh my?"

The Kurumi in his head gasped, and the face of the Kurumi before
his eyes relaxed into a smile.

"I'm honored to receive such praise. Well then, we will meet again in
five years," she said finally, taking control of the gun that was shaking
with the incredible Spirit power it contained.

She pulled the trigger, and an inky-black line was drawn from the
barrel to his chest.

The instant Yud Bet hit, Shido felt his own body twist into a spiral, pulled into the rotation of the bullet. And then his field of view was swallowed up by a vortex before going completely black.

◇

"*...do, Shido.*"

"...!" Hearing his name in his head, Shido snapped his eyes open with a gasp. A heartbeat later, he realized he was lying flat on his back on the roof of the same building he'd blacked out on. On second thought, calling it the same building wasn't entirely accurate. There was no sign of the other Kurumi, and more than anything else, he could see no hint of flames flickering up from the ground in the Nanko district.

"Did...it work?" he asked himself.

"*It appears so, hmm?*" Kurumi responded.

Although he didn't know exactly what time it was, he had indeed gone back to the past once more. To a world before the fire, a world before Kotori became a Spirit, a world before Origami accidentally killed her parents.

"*You don't have time to wallow in emotion, Shido,*" Kurumi chided him.

"Yeah...I know." He stood up and then looked again at Nanko spreading out below him. He clenched his hands into fists. "Let's go change the world," he said, a rallying call to the Kurumi who was nothing more than a voice in his head.

Kurumi paused like her voice had caught in her throat for a second. "*Yes,*" she replied at last.

Shido leaped into the stairwell and started racing down the emergency stairs. "It's great that I managed to get back to before the fire started, but what am I supposed to do now?"

"*You were off to such an excellent and stylish start, and now you're ruining it.*" Her voice was somehow icy.

"Hngh! I—I mean, I gotta ask!" he cried. "And, like, you sound a whole lot colder than before?"

"*I sound like I always sound,*" she said sulkily.

Had he said something to upset her? And then it hit him.

"Kurumi, is it maybe that eye patch?"

"*In any case,*" she said, as if to shut him up. "*If you merely run around at random, you'll only end up with the same result as before. The difference between now and before is that we know what's going to happen. That's it. With that in mind, let's take stock of the situation.*"

"O-okay..."

"*First of all, what is it that we must accomplish?*" she asked in a teacherly tone, and Shido set his brain to work as he kept descending the stairs at top speed.

"I guess that'd be not letting Origami kill her parents," he said.

"*Yes, that's exactly correct,*" she agreed. "*So what can you do to make that happen, Shido?*"

He frowned. "Uh. We stop her... Do whatever it takes?"

"*That is indeed the most obvious plan, but I doubt it's very realistic.*"

"Hngh." He groaned and screwed up his face. "I—I guess not."

Origami believed that Phantom had killed her parents; she was vengeance personified at the moment. It was doubtful she'd even notice Shido, regardless of what he tried. Not to mention that now that she was a Spirit, she had almost boundless power. It had been all Shido could do to simply follow her as she fought that dizzying midair battle against Phantom.

Naturally, there was still a slim chance he could stop her. The idea that Origami would eventually notice Shido and listen to him wasn't entirely implausible. But she also had a very limited amount of time here—the effects of Yud Bet would wear off sooner than later. Most likely, this would be his last chance at a do-over. It was too risky to wager everything on such an optimistic hope.

"In that case," he said. "What do you think about getting Origami's parents to a safe place?"

"*Interesting,*" Kurumi mused. "*That might be more viable than engaging Origami herself.*"

"R-right? So then—"

"*But there is an issue,*" she interrupted. "*I wonder if they would be willing to listen to a strange boy on their doorstep telling them they're in danger and they have to flee.*"

"I-I'll explain the sit—"

"*You'd tell them you come from the future and they're about to be killed by their time-traveling daughter, and they have to believe you?*"

"Unh…" He broke out in a sweat.

The reason the past Kurumi had believed him when he came to her for help was partly because of her own ability to reverse time, but mostly it was because of the presence of future Kurumi's voice in his head. If he tried to explain what was happening to Origami's parents when they didn't even know that Spirits existed, he'd still be talking when the fire broke out.

"*Also,*" Kurumi continued. "*Even if everything goes perfectly smoothly, and you do manage to evacuate her parents, you still don't know whether or not that will really set everything on the right path.*"

"Huh?" He furrowed his brow. "Wh-what do you mean?"

"*If the world is actively trying to correct any deviations, then Origami's beam of light could come down wherever you bring her parents, now couldn't it?*"

"…!" He was at a loss for words. It was true. Kurumi was exactly right. From the moment that he'd gone back in time, he had changed events ever so slightly from the world he and his friends knew. It was dangerous to assume that everything would go exactly as it had in his memory.

But something wasn't clicking for him. He narrowed his eyes suspiciously. "Kurumi. Didn't you reject the idea of history's power to correct itself?"

"*My word!*" She gasped. "*I have no recollection of rejecting anything. I merely posed the question of whether the concept had actually been proved.*"

"…" He had a feeling that she was just blowing smoke, but now was not the time for that discussion. He shook his head to focus. "Okay then, what are you saying I should do?"

"Yes, that is the question, hmm?" Kurumi fell silent for a moment, as if giving it some thought. *"How about you prevent Origami from realizing that she is the one who killed her parents?"*

"Huh?" he cried. "Wh-what are you even talking about!"

"Goodness, I do think this makes surprising sense, though," she said. *"Origami inverted because she discovered that the one who tragically changed her life forever turned out to be herself, yes?"*

"Th-that's true, but then the fact that she killed her parents won't change!" Shido couldn't stop himself from shouting.

It was true that if he did what she suggested, he might be able to keep Origami from inverting. But that wouldn't change the fact that she had murdered her own parents. And it also wouldn't change that her parents had died at the hands of a Spirit, leaving Origami with an all-consuming desire for vengeance that would be turned on someone else. On Kotori, who started the fire, or on Phantom, who gave her that power.

"Oh…," he said, quietly, once his train of thought reached this point.

"Hmm? Is something the matter?" the Kurumi in his head said. *"You're not moving anymore."*

He realized he'd unconsciously stopped in his tracks. But before he could get his feet going again, the thought that had popped up in his head was making its way out of his mouth.

"Hey, Kurumi?"

"What is it?"

"Basically, so long as there's no enemy there when Origami shows up…it's all good, right?"

Five minutes later, Shido was hiding in the bushes at the park, staring at a little girl with her hair up in pigtails, sitting on a swing. She was maybe seven or eight years old, and her sweet face was clouded over in sadness as she pumped her legs listlessly, making the swing chains squeak.

There was no doubt about it. This was his little sister five years earlier.

"Kotori…" He felt a fist squeeze his heart when he looked at her somber expression. Today had been her birthday. He'd gone to the next station over to buy her a present so he could surprise her. He never imagined she'd felt so sad and alone on this day.

While his heart ached at the sight of her, a giggle echoed inside his head.

"*Shido, if I didn't know any better, I'd think you're quite the pervert,*" Kurumi remarked.

"Shut up," he replied in a low voice. He had already been worried about that very thing. If anyone had come across a teenage boy peeping from the shrubbery at a little girl, there would have been immediate outcry, and pamphlets about the potential criminal would undoubtedly be circulated in the neighborhood the following day, urging caution.

But he wasn't trying to preserve this precious, fleeting moment of the young Kotori by burning it into his retinas. Shido was waiting for Phantom to show up.

"*This is quite impetuous of you, Shido,*" Kurumi said, sounding amused.

"I—I…," Shido stammered. "I didn't have a lot of other options, okay? Besides, you agreed this plan could work, Kurumi."

"*Well, that is true. If you can chase off Phantom before Origami arrives, then Origami will indeed no longer have a target to attack.*"

"If possible," he said, half to himself. "I'd like to talk to her, though."

"*Talk? With Phantom?*" Kurumi asked, sounding slightly surprised. "*That's unexpected. I was certain you were hostile toward Phantom.*"

"Well, yeah," he said. "I can't deny that I've felt that way sometimes. We're talking about the reason Kotori and whoever else became Spirits. But I don't know anything about Phantom. If I just make up my mind without even giving talking a chance, then I'm no better than all those people who see Tohka and Yoshino as nothing more than disasters."

Kurumi was silent for a while, as if exasperated. Finally, she burst out laughing, like she couldn't hold it in for another second. *"Hee! Hee-hee! Ha-ha-ha-ha!"*

"Wh-what?" He glared into empty air.

"Oh, I merely thought how very Shido *that idea is."* She laughed again and then continued. *"But I really don't recommend attempting to strike up a conversation. Phantom is quite difficult to get ahold of. And given how much of a bleeding heart you are, it can only end with you getting deceived one way or the other."*

"Huh? Kurumi, do you know—?" Shido cut himself off.

The reason was simple. A curious visitor had appeared in his field of view, at the feet of Kotori playing alone in the park. A *something* with no discernible age, gender, or physique. But that was only natural. *It* was covered in what appeared to be static, which concealed every aspect of its appearance.

Phantom. The being responsible for turning Kotori, Miku, and Origami into Spirits. That was who stood in front of Kotori now.

"…!" Eyes glued to Phantom, Shido felt goose bumps on his skin. In the back of his mind, he recalled the pained look on Kotori's face after she became the Spirit Efreet.

"Shido, you mustn't get ahead of yourself," Kurumi warned.

"…Yeah. I know." He exhaled slowly to get his racing heart under control and hugged himself to stop shaking. Drops of blood welled up where his fingernails dug into his upper arms.

He must not stop Kotori from turning into a Spirit. Kurumi had been very clear about this when they'd discussed the plan.

Kotori and Phantom conversed briefly, and then the Spirit held out what looked to be a red gem. The moment Kotori touched it, her body shone faintly.

"Ah. Ah! Aaaaaaaaaah!" she cried out in agony.

At the same time, an intense wave of heat swirled up around her, and flames roared to life.

"Ngh!" Shido crouched, held his breath, and somehow managed to endure the blast of hot air. When he timidly opened his eyes a few seconds later, Kotori was clad in a Japanese-style Astral Dress.

She had become the Spirit of flames, Efreet.

"Kotori...I'm sorry," he murmured, pained, and then narrowed his eyes sharply. "...!"

Mustering up his courage, he leaped out of the bushes behind the mass of static standing in front of Kotori.

"Hey!" he called, his voice tense.

"...Hmm?" Phantom said in a voice that showed no hint of gender. The hazy, pixelated blur standing in his field of view seemed to move ever so slightly. Apparently, Phantom had turned toward Shido and was looking his way.

He exhaled slowly and glared at the part that probably corresponded to Phantom's face. "'Sup? I've been wanting to meet you, Phantom." He spoke the name of the static in a quiet voice.

His words were not sarcastic. Ever since he'd resealed Kotori's power and gotten his memories of the incident five years ago back, somewhere in his heart had lurked the desire to meet this mysterious being again, the monster that audaciously wielded the extremely supernatural and irrational ability to make a human a Spirit. The culprit that had turned Kotori, Miku, and Origami into Spirits and had sown chaos and destruction in the world. Shido felt a deep connection, something like destiny, with the *something* that had changed his life.

But the words Phantom spoke to him were completely unexpected.

"...Huh?" they said quietly, and shuddered.

Naturally, their body was still covered in static, so to his eyes, this looked like nothing more than the distorted movement of pixelated space. But for some reason, he couldn't help but feel that this movement came from some kind of astonishment or confusion.

Of course, this was a perfectly natural reaction, given that he had come out of nowhere and called out to the being. But that wasn't it. Phantom's reaction was clearly a different type of surprise.

"...This can't— You... Why are you...?"

"Huh?" Shido frowned dubiously. "Do you...*know* me?"

"..." Phantom said nothing. But it didn't seem like the being was ignoring his question or trying not to give him any unnecessary information. To Shido, it looked like they had been stunned into silence.

He frowned. He understood the whole thing even less now. It was hard to square the detached, aloof Phantom in his memory and what he was seeing now. He could almost believe that it was a completely different person on the other side of the static.

"......" Without any warning, Phantom started running away, gliding across the earth.

"*Shido.*"

"Got it!" Shido started chasing after Phantom, spurred on by Kurumi's voice.

For an instant, his eyes stopped on Kotori, slumped on the ground in the park. The little girl had just obtained unfathomable power, and now she was wailing, "Shiiidooo! Shiiidooo!"

"...! Hngh!" Even though his heart threatened to rip in two, he steeled himself and kept going. If memory served, his past Shido would be coming along soon. He couldn't exactly afford to run into himself here. And more than anything else, he couldn't let Phantom get away. If he wasn't careful, he'd lose sight of that mass of static. He urged his legs to move faster.

He'd succeeded in getting the Spirit away from the park, but that alone wouldn't be enough. His and Kurumi's objective was to keep the future Origami from seeing Phantom. To accomplish this, he had to make the static Spirit go somewhere Origami wouldn't find them—he had to make her Lost to the parallel world.

"*Her reaction was quite unexpected, hmm?*" Kurumi's voice echoed in his head as he pursued Phantom. "*Shido, do you know that person?*"

"...! As far as I know, I don't know anyone who's totally pixelated!" he shouted, racing through the burning streets.

"*Hmm... I suppose,*" Kurumi replied, sounding somehow uninterested.

And he was telling the truth. He'd encountered Phantom just the one time, five years ago. Although that "five years ago" was right now.

Despite what he remembered, Phantom very clearly knew him. And he had met someone else who evinced a similar reaction upon seeing his face—DEM Industries Managing Director, Isaac Westcott.

When Shido had broken into DEM's Japan office to rescue Tohka after she was abducted, Westcott had grinned broadly upon seeing him, even though they had supposedly never met. And when he left, he'd called Shido "Takamiya."

"...!" His heart pounded in a way totally divorced from the intense exercise.

Takamiya. The same last name as Mana Takamiya, who insisted she was his biological sister. And he had no memories from before he was adopted by the Itsuka family.

"My... I bet Phantom knows something!" he cried out as he chased the Spirit fleeing through the city sunk into flame.

Now that he was thinking about it, there were a number of things he didn't know: What had he been doing before he was taken in by the Itsukas? Why had Westcott recognized him? What exactly *was* the power he had anyway, the power to seal Spirits?

He'd locked away the powers of seven Spirits, who he now shared his life with, but he still didn't know the answers to any of these questions.

"Ngh..." Shido gritted his teeth in frustration and pushed himself to run even faster.

Ahead of him, Phantom abruptly stopped in their tracks. He followed suit and brought himself to a forceful stop.

"...! Phantom!" he called.

"..." Phantom's static-covered body swayed. They had apparently turned around.

"...Phantom? So that's the name I've been given," they murmured, as though processing the information, before sighing. "...Sorry for suddenly running away from you. I just thought it would be better to not do this in front of her."

The "her" was most likely Kotori.

He still didn't understand Phantom's intentions, but it was true that this way *was* better for him. If he'd stayed in the park, past Shido and the Spiritified Origami would have come along eventually.

"..." Phantom fell silent, standing in place. Apparently, they were taking a good look at Shido. "...Aah, okay. It really is you." They made a gesture like a small nod, as if they were finally convinced. At the same time, the film of static vanished like mist.

"Wha...?" Shido's eyes flew open.

A girl emerged from the static. She had braided hair and the look of an affectionate mother on her face. Shido felt his head spinning. Something about her face made him feel strange. He couldn't shake the feeling that he'd seen her somewhere, despite also being certain they'd never met before.

"You're..." He gaped.

"...I can't yet let you see my real self, so apologies for this provisional form. But now that I finally get to speak with you, I'd rather not do it through a barrier," Phantom replied, sounding girlish and clear, a change from her voice up to that point.

Provisional form. So this girl wasn't actually Phantom? But why would she go to such lengths...?

Shido's mind raced, and Phantom's cherry-pink lips curled up in a gentle smile.

"...*When* exactly did you come from?" she asked. "From looking at you, I'd say five or six years from now?"

"Ngh! How...?" His jaw dropped. He never imagined that Phantom would not only know him but also figure out that he'd traveled back in time.

"..." Kurumi was as cool as ever, however. It almost seemed like she'd anticipated this conversation.

"...So...what do you want?" Phantom continued, her voice quiet. "You went so far as to use a bullet of time reversal to come to this era. You're not going to tell me it was just for sightseeing, right?"

"..."

Shido glanced to his rear at the park where he and Phantom had been. Still no shining Spirit in the sky above it. After confirming this, he opened his mouth. "Do you...*know* me?"

"…Mm-hmm, I do. Pretty well," she replied, and his heart leaped into his throat.

"Tell me," he demanded. "What…*am* I exactly? What is this power?"

"…" Phantom fell silent for a few seconds. She shook her head slightly before replying. "…I do want to answer that for you. But given that I don't know what's happening with future you, I can't. And there might be someone listening in on us now."

"Huh…?" His eyes grew wide, and Phantom continued as if she had seen right through him.

"Say…Kurumi Tokisaki?" she said. "You can hear me, right?"

"*Oh my, oh dear,*" Kurumi said quietly inside Shido's head.

"…Is that all you wanted?" Phantom asked. "If it is, this is quite the decadent use of 'time.'"

Shido lowered his eyes and shook his head. "No. That was just a question I had. I need something else from you."

"…And what's that?" She looked at him curiously.

"Disappear from here right now."

There were a ton of other things he wanted to ask. He'd finally found someone who knew his past. He was dying to know more. If he was honest, he wanted to do whatever it took to find out something about himself. But what he *needed* right now was for her to go. He had to prioritize preventing Origami's inversion.

"…Is this a poetic way of saying you're going to kill me?" Phantom sighed wearily. "Well… It's not like this is completely out of left field. It was a possibility that you would land on this way of thinking if a certain difficult Spirit of time were to favor this future, although it's one I didn't really want to think about."

"…"

Phantom apparently thought that he had traveled through time to kill her. He silently clenched his hands into fists.

He would have been lying if he claimed to feel no hostility toward Phantom. He still couldn't forgive the pain she'd caused baby Kotori. But at the moment, he had no interest in doing anything in particular to her. After taking a deep breath to calm himself, he shook his head.

"I never said anything about killing. I just want you to get out of here right now. You *can* go to the parallel world, right?"

"...Hmm?" Phantom looked at him with keen interest. "Can I ask the reason?"

"It-it's...," Shido stammered.

He knew far too little about the thought process and objectives of the girl before him. It would have been easy to say that Origami, a girl Phantom turned into a Spirit five years in the future, was coming back to this time to attack her. And it would have been simple to inform her of his desire to prevent Origami's inversion. But if Phantom's goal was the same as DEM's Isaac Westcott's—to make the Spirits invert—then handing over that information would have the exact opposite effect.

"..."

How exactly should he respond? When he was failing to make that decision, Phantom sighed, as if frustrated.

"...Well, if you can't answer, that's fine. Either way, I'm sorry, but the answer is no. I still have a little something left to do here."

"Wha...?!" He was stunned at this response. "Hang on! In this timeline—" Shido opened his mouth to tell her about Origami. But before he could, his body froze, unable to move, as though an invisible hand were pressing down on him. It felt very similar to the way his body had been bound by Territories deployed by AST or DEM Wizards. He could barely move his fingertips, and he definitely couldn't speak.

"*Shido, what is the matter?*" Kurumi asked suspiciously, but he couldn't answer her.

Phantom slowly approached him. She raised a hand to his cheek.

"...?!" An indescribable sensation shot through his body. "Ah—"

He didn't know why. But he was certain he *recognized* this sensation. He knew this *something* that had taken the form of a girl.

"...Maybe I should be grateful to the Spirit of time's action today,"

Phantom said quietly, her hand still on his cheek. "When the moment is right, we'll meet again. And when we do…"

"I'll never let you go. I won't make that mistake again."

"…?!" He gasped unconsciously. He didn't know where. He didn't know when. But he was sure he'd heard those words before.

"…"

He tried to ask *Who are you?* but his voice refused to come out.

Phantom pulled her hand away from his cheek and enveloped herself in static again before launching herself from the ground and flying into the sky.

A few seconds later, when Phantom was far beyond his reach no matter how high he might have jumped, the invisible force that bound him finally slackened.

"Ngh. Hah! *Koff! Koff!*" He fell to his knees and gasped for breath. But now was not the time for that. He immediately turned his face toward the sky. "What is she…?"

At that exact moment, a beam of light shot forward from the east toward Phantom floating in the sky.

"…! She—!" He shuddered, turned his face toward the source of light, and froze on the spot.

Snowy-white, luminescent Astral Dress. A number of feathers pointing at the enemy, like a physical manifestation of the desire to kill. An angel spreading the light of destruction. It went without saying; he was looking at Origami Tobiichi herself.

"Origami!" Shido shrieked her name.

But there was no way for his voice to reach her. Origami was entirely focused on Phantom, shooting a wall of lasers from the tips of her feather-shaped Angel.

Phantom slid through the sky, dodging every blow with impossible agility. But Origami didn't give up. She doggedly pursued the other Spirit who was trying to flee, sending a shower of light beams into the air.

He was watching exactly the same scene as earlier, before he'd gotten the past Kurumi to send him back in time a second time.

Kurumi's earlier words flitted through his head. *If the world is actively trying to correct any deviations, then…*

"Dammit!" He shook his head, as if to shake off the resignation that started to bob up inside him, and started running, chasing after the battle in the sky. "Like I'm gonna…let it happen again!"

The images of what he'd witnessed before filled his mind. The light pouring down from the sky. The scattered human remains. And the eyes of a little girl colored with hatred and a hunger for vengeance.

Origami was only trying to save her parents. She was just trying to fight cruel destiny. That noble desire couldn't be allowed to give birth to such tragedy…

"I *will* change it!" he shouted and pushed his legs to move even faster.

There was no way he could hope to keep up with Origami and Phantom as they shot through the air above at such tremendous speed. But tracking them precisely wasn't his goal. Without hesitation, he proceeded into the town engulfed in flames. And soon he reached his destination. The spot where Origami's parents had died in the previous world.

Yes. What Shido needed to stop was not the battle between Origami and Phantom but Origami's stray attack.

"…! Found you!" He opened his eyes wide as he ran through the brightly burning streets.

He had spotted the younger Origami and her parents slightly ahead of her.

There was no time left to talk. Now that he'd failed to prevent Origami and Phantom from making contact, the only way he could change the past was to get Origami's parents away to a safe place.

Perhaps this was a silver lining. The town was currently on fire. A boy urging them to hurry and evacuate would not be out of place. It was much more likely they would heed his warning and flee.

But.

"…! Wha—?" His eyes grew as big as saucers, and his whole body stiffened.

The reason was extremely simple. At some point, the Spirits Origami and Phantom had appeared in the sky directly above Origami's parents. Apparently, their fight had already progressed to this fateful moment.

"Ngh!" Shido gritted his teeth in frustration. Origami released several beams of light to block Phantom's path of escape. Then she gathered the feathers of her Angel in one cluster and aimed them toward the ground. Just like before.

His face drained of color. "Origami! You can't!" he shouted, but she couldn't hear him, of course.

He no longer had the option of urging her parents to flee. In another second, the fatal blow would land, and they would be dead before they even had a chance to feel anything.

"Dammit!!" He pushed himself even further and pumped his legs as hard as he could.

Shido?! Kurumi's surprised voice echoed inside his head. She had apparently not expected him to do this.

But he couldn't think of any other way.

The composite Angel shot a tremendous pillar of light toward the ground.

"Aaaaaaaaaaaaaaaaaaah!" At the same time, Shido yelled loud enough to make his throat bleed and leaped toward Origami's parents, pushing them aside with every ounce of strength left in his body.

"Wha—?!"

"Eeeaaah!"

Origami's mother and father both cried out when they were abruptly sent flying by the hard impact. They might have ended up skinning their knees or getting bruised, but he was sure they would forgive him this much.

He'd definitely chosen the stupidest way to do this, if he did say so himself. The corners of his mouth turned up in a self-deprecating smile as his vision started going white.

"…!"

He heard a voice. He thought it was maybe Kurumi at first, only to realize it wasn't her. The voice wasn't coming from inside his head. And just as everything in his field of view was on the verge of being consumed by light, Shido figured out that it was the voice of the Origami from five years ago.

For a moment, their eyes met. He couldn't see any burning desire for vengeance there. She was not trapped in a cage of hatred.

"Aah, thank goodness," he murmured before he was enveloped in pure white light and consciousness slipped away.

Chapter 8
Devil

"Nnn." Shido opened his eyes with a groan. He had been lying face-down on a bed, his left cheek pressed into a pillow, forcing him to keep his left eye closed. His left arm seemed to have been pinned under his body for some time; he had lost all feeling in it.

"Haah…" After yawning sleepily, he rolled onto his back and sat up. The moment it was freed from his own body weight, his arm that had fallen asleep began to tingle and prickle. He screwed up his face with an "Ow-ow-ow!" and then looked around absently.

There was nothing particularly noteworthy. He was in his own bedroom, which looked like it always did. Familiar walls, floor, ceiling, furniture. Maybe he'd been especially tired the day before, since his school uniform blazer was unusually draped over the back of a chair.

"Huh…?" He blinked rapidly. Something was off. He had absolutely no memory of how he'd gotten to bed last night. And what day, what date, what month was it even? Before he went to sleep, he was pretty sure he—

"…!" The dots connected one after the other in his head, and he recalled the last thing he saw before he lost consciousness. The town in flames. Light beams shooting from the sky.

He looked down at himself with a gasp. From what he could tell, he had no visible burns or missing limbs. Even though he was 100 percent certain he'd been hit with the unparalleled power of Origami's Angel, he was the picture of health. Maybe it was thanks to Kotori's healing flames, or maybe Yud Bet had worn off the instant he was about to be burned up by the light, forcibly returning him to his original place in time.

Well, either way, it was clear that he'd managed to escape from the jaws of death. He let out a huge sigh of relief.

But the next question immediately popped up in his head. He hurriedly got out of bed, drew the curtains, and opened the windows.

"Is it…?" he murmured as he looked out at the world.

Spreading out before him was the familiar residential neighborhood of east Tengu. He glanced to his right and found the massive apartment building where the Spirits lived.

"Kurumi! Kurumi!" He pressed a hand to the side of his head and spoke to the Spirit inside it. But no matter how long he waited, he didn't hear a reply.

That was the expected result. Kurumi had said that Tet was a bullet that let her connect to the mind of a target in a different time. Meaning that the effect wouldn't work on someone who existed in the same time as the Kurumi who fired the bullet.

Yes. Shido had returned from the Tengu of five years earlier.

"Wait…" He half spat the word. That wasn't quite right.

What he saw was utterly familiar and unchanged from the usual. The houses crammed together, the streets… Everything seemed perfectly normal. In other words, this was not a Tengu that had been completely ripped apart by an inverted Origami.

"…!" He left his room, window still open, and practically rolled down the stairs in his excitement. He raced into the living room and threw the door open with a bang.

And this was perhaps a surprise. The small girl sitting on the sofa and watching TV in the living room—Kotori—looked at him with eyes that were already the size of acorns and were now open even wider.

"Uh? What's up, Big Bro?" she said nonchalantly. "You sure are energetic first thing in the morning." She was a lively girl with long hair tied up in white ribbons. She'd apparently gotten up much earlier than he had; she was already dressed in her school uniform.

"Kotori!" he cried breathlessly. "You're okay?!"

"…Huh?" She cocked her head to one side, like she had no idea what he was on about. "Are you still asleep?"

He gasped. But he couldn't help his outburst. In his original world, *Fraxinus* had been downed by Origami, and he hadn't been able to find out if Kotori and her crew on board had survived.

"Kotori, what's the date today?" he asked.

"Huh? November eighth. Duh," she replied, looking at him with concern.

But her reaction was the best possible news for him. If he remembered right, that was the day *after* the inverted Origami destroyed the city.

"Aaah." He walked over to her, almost in tears, and threw his arms around her. She was baffled by the suddenness of it all.

"Eeaugh?!" she shrieked

"Kotori," he said. "Kotori! I'm so glad. You're really—"

"Eeaah! Augh!" She flailed wildly, hitting him with a kick to the gut, and he dropped to his knees.

But right now, even that pain was a reason to celebrate. He was overwhelmed by a sense of achievement and relief.

"What's wrong? You're being weird, Shido," Kotori said, hugging herself, her cheeks reddening. And from her perspective, having lived in the revised world for the last five years, his behavior could have only seemed odd.

"Hey, Kotori?" he said from the floor. "If I told you I accidentally changed the world yesterday, would you believe me?"

"Huh?" She opened her eyes wide and then furrowed her brow. "What're you talking about? You delusional?" she said, running a finger along her jawline. She looked less like she didn't believe him and more like she had no idea what he was talking about.

But that was all right.

A wry grin sprang onto his face as he waved his hand at her. "Mm. Sorry. I guess I was still half asleep there. Hang on a sec. I'll whip something up for breakfast."

"O-okay." She nodded, a dubious look on her face.

Shrugging slightly, Shido headed for the washroom to clean his face. At some point, he'd have to give her a report about the changes to their timeline. The key piece of information was that he'd literally over-written the world. He couldn't exactly not tell Ratatoskr about this, considering the implications.

But how on earth would he explain his experiences when they sounded like a far-fetched dream? He scratched his cheek and groaned.

He had breakfast with Kotori and finished getting ready for school. Leaving the house, he caught sight of a familiar face already waiting at the gate.

"Oh, there you are, Shido! It's morning!" The beautiful girl with hair the color of night and eyes like crystals waved her hand vigorously. Tohka Yatogami, his classmate and neighbor.

"Hey, Tohka," he greeted her. "Morning. Sorry. Were you waiting?"

"No, I just got here a second ago," she said, beaming. "It's perfect!"

Shido couldn't help but laugh at her innocent air.

"Mm?" She frowned. "What's wrong?"

"Oh, nothing. Anyway, here," he said, handing her the lunch bag he was holding. He generally made her lunch, together with his and Kotori's in the morning. He'd gotten up late that day, though, so he'd thought they might have to just buy something. But he'd hurried to prepare their lunches, wanting to get a little closer to his usual routine for the first time in a long time.

"Ooh!" She clapped her hands together. "Thank you, Shido! Today's the day, right? The little cutlet bits are in here?"

Now it was Shido's turn to cock his head in confusion. "Huh?"

"Mm? It's not?" Tohka frowned and put a finger to her chin as if remembering. "I feel like that's what you said when we said good-bye yesterday."

Shido suddenly understood that he had no memory of saying anything like that, but it was very likely that was indeed what Tohka had heard.

This world was the one where he'd saved Origami's parents five years earlier and Origami hadn't inverted. Thus, Tengu hadn't been destroyed, and yesterday had been an utterly ordinary day for Shido and his friends. But having been five years in the past until just a few hours earlier, he had no recollection of this world before yesterday.

From his interactions with Tohka and Kotori, there didn't seem to be any big changes from his original world, but there were bound to be other details like this one that he didn't know. Maybe the best thing to do was to check in with everyone as soon as he possibly could.

"Oh," he said. "Sorry, Tohka. I didn't have the ingredients for that. I made something else."

"Mm. You did? But you don't need to apologize. Everything you make is yummy! So then, what is it?"

"Oh, minced meat, scrambled eggs, greens, and rice. I made the egg on the sweet side."

"Wh-what...?! This is totally the best!" she said excitedly, cheeks flushing. Apparently, she was pleased with the revised menu.

When she danced off, clutching her lunch bag to her chest, he saw two other girls walking his way from the apartment building.

"Kah-kah, a splendid morn. You fulfilled your responsibility to come for me, servant."

"Bow. Good morning, Shido, Tohka."

Kaguya Yamai and Yuzuru Yamai, twin girls with identical faces. They looked so much alike that it seemed impossible to tell them apart at a glance. But if you looked closely, you could see differences in the way they wore their hair, slight changes in their expressions, and tragically different physiques that could have only been a prank played by some god.

"Hmm? Were you not at this moment thinking something extremely rude?" The girl with the daring expression—Kaguya—narrowed her eyes at him as she hugged her own shoulders protectively.

He hurried to shake his head. "A-as if. I wasn't thinking anything."

"Do you speak truth? It is a great crime to present falsehoods to me, you know?"

"Advice. You're overthinking, Kaguya." Now the glamorous girl with her hair in braids—Yuzuru—spoke and set a hand on her sister's shoulder.

"Be that as it may." Kaguya sniffed. "I witnessed the eyes of Shido travel between the bosoms of myself and Yuzuru, albeit for a mere instant."

"Explanation. This is a conditioned reflex for a boy."

"…Hey." He rolled his eyes as a bead of sweat rolled down his cheek. He was quickly finding it impossible to keep up with them.

"Aah. Which is to say that his body reacted to our allure? If that is the case, then perhaps I shall be forgiving. Likely nothing in this world is more arduous than resisting the Yamai allure."

"Assent. That's exactly right. You may fantasize incorrectly about Shido on a daily basis, but why would anyone be thinking about you that way?"

"I—I am not engaging in such fantasies!" Kaguya shouted, turning beet red.

"Smile. Pffft!" Yuzuru put a hand to her mouth as if delighting in her reaction. "Dubious. Is that true? Then the diary entry you wrote last night—"

"Hey! Ah! Aaaaaaaah!" Kaguya started yelling and screaming and whapping Yuzuru's shoulder.

"Flight. Eeek!" Yuzuru said, sounding not very frightened at all, and ran away. Kaguya immediately gave chase, and the girls began to run circles around Shido.

"Ha-ha-ha!" He couldn't help but laugh.

Kaguya and Yuzuru both got curious looks on their faces at this reaction to their shenanigans.

"Wh-what, Shido? You appear quite composed all of a sudden."

"Assent. It is as though you aged overnight."

Both girls furrowed their brows and turned pensive gazes at him. He wedged himself in between them and shook his head to try to change the subject.

"No, it's nothing," he said. "Anyway, c'mon. We can't stand around here forever. We're gonna be late."

Kaguya and Yuzuru looked at each other before sighing simultaneously and shrugging.

"Hmph. I am taken aback. In deference to Shido, I shall have mercy on you as a special favor," Kaguya declared. "But there will be no next time. Any who would expose our darkness should know the hand of the god of death will be upon them soon enough."

"Sneer. 'Our darkness.'" Yuzuru rolled her eyes. "Ha-ha! Is the darkness that thing you hide under your bed, Kaguya?"

"Wh—?! How did you know about thaaaaaat?!"

"Dash. I'll be on my way." Yuzuru waved at Shido and Tohka, and ran off toward the school.

"Haaaaalt! Huh? No, but seriously?! How do you knooooooow?!" Kaguya chased after her, shrieking. Although their power had been locked away, these sisters were indeed still Spirits of the wind; they disappeared from sight soon enough.

"How about we get going, too?" Shido asked with a shrug.

"Mm?" Tohka blinked a few times before nodding in return. "Mm-hmm, okay!"

And then they walked down the road to school side by side until they reached the high school.

Shido slipped through the gates, changed into his indoor shoes, went down the hallway and up the stairs, and came to stand in front of Grade 11, Class 4.

"..."

But just as he was about to reach out for the classroom door, he stopped.

The reason was simple. He didn't know whether or not he should speak to the girl who sat at the desk to the left of his own. Origami.

Without a doubt, she would have been the one most affected by the change five years earlier. Maybe the discrepancy in their memories wouldn't be a small one, like with Tohka that morning, but some even larger change.

"Shido, you're not going in?" Tohka asked.

"Uh. Yeah… Sorry." He reached out and set a hand on the door. And then, with a strange mix of anxiety and gloom, he opened it.

But.

"Huh?" He looked in on the class and sighed, smiling faintly.

There was no one sitting at the desk to the left of his own. It seemed that Origami hadn't arrived yet.

He felt a little embarrassed at having steeled himself to face her. He scratched his cheek as he took his seat and got his books for first period out of his bag.

He kept waiting, checking the clock, but Origami was still nowhere to be seen.

"Mm." Tohka abruptly got a troubled look on her face.

"Hmm?" He looked over at her. "What's up, Tohka?"

"Mm." She cocked her head to one side curiously. "I just sort of have this feeling like something's missing or… It's weird."

"Something's missing?" He stared at her. But before he could press her for details, the bell rang to indicate the start of the day.

Not long after, the classroom door opened and a small woman wearing glasses came inside carrying the attendance register. Their homeroom teacher, Tama, aka Ms. Tamae Okamine.

When Shido saw her, his face unconsciously relaxed into a smile. Because she was basically unchanged from how she'd looked when he'd encountered her five years in the past.

"Itsuka?" she said, raising a dubious eyebrow. "Do I have something on my face?"

"…! Oh. No," he replied hurriedly. "Uh. Sorry."

She cleared her throat, as if to collect herself, and began taking attendance. Since his last name was Itsuka, he was not so far from the top of the list. Soon, he was answering that he was in fact here, and then he turned his gaze to the empty desk at his side.

"Origami," he murmured.

She hadn't shown up even after the start of homeroom. Was she absent today? Or was she just late, although that was unusual for her?

Even while he mulled this over, Tama continued to call out the names of the other students. "All right. Tonomachi is here, so then." She paused to look down at the register. "Next, is Nakahara?"

"Huh?" Shido automatically let out a baffled cry.

But that was no wonder. If she was going in order of the attendance roster, alternating boy-girl-boy-girl, then it was weird that Origami Tobiichi didn't come after Hiroto Tonomachi. Even if she wasn't there, that was no reason not to call her name.

"Hmm?" Tama looked at him in surprise. He'd apparently been louder than he thought. "Did I make a mistake?"

"Uh. Oh…" He stood up, his chair clattering. But he hesitated to say what he was thinking out loud. A thought flashed through his brain, a memory of the time when Origami had supposedly transferred schools in his original world.

If he didn't say anything, though, he wouldn't learn what had happened. Firming his resolve, he opened his mouth. "What happened to…Origami?"

His heart pounded in his chest. In his original world, Origami's "transfer" had been the cover story after she'd been headhunted by DEM Industries. But that wouldn't have happened to the Origami of this world, since she wouldn't have the same hatred of the Spirits. He knew this, and yet he held his breath, expecting Tama to confirm his fear. "Tobiichi transferred schools, didn't she?"

But Tama's response was entirely different from the one he'd braced himself for.

"Origami…?" Tama said, looking baffled. "Who would that be exactly?"

*　　*　　*

"Wha—?" His eyes grew wide, and he looked around. Because he'd stood up so suddenly to ask the question, the eyes of everyone in class were currently turned toward him. And all their faces showed the same puzzlement.

"Origami? What's that?" he heard someone say. "A person's name?"

"Itsuka's folding origami cranes for Tama?" another questioned.

"No, that's only if she was in the hospital. And I mean, you can't do the thousand cranes by yourself."

"No, but I mean, Itsuka could."

"Hmm. Yeah."

Shido looked around at his classmates as he felt his breathing gradually grow more ragged. They didn't appear to be joking. None of them knew the girl Origami Tobiichi.

"Ohhh. I. Guess." He took a shallow breath. The strength drained from his body, and his hands dropped to his sides.

Now that he was forced to think about it, something like this wasn't unthinkable. It was plenty possible. But somewhere in his head, he had maybe been trying to avoid considering it.

If the young Origami had survived the catastrophe with her parents, then it made sense that they would have found a new house and moved. They might still have been living in the Nanko district, or they might have moved to a different area, like the Itsuka family. In which case, there was no guarantee she would have been enrolled at Raizen High School together with Shido in the first place.

Five years earlier, he had changed history. He had succeeded in erasing the tragedy in his world before it happened. But that didn't necessarily mean that all of history had been revised in line with his expectations. Every event in the world was connected by an invisible line. His success was a new starting point, and it was inevitable that other changes would occur, changes that were well beyond his original objective.

"I'm sorry, Ms. Okamine. My mistake. Please continue," he said quietly, and almost collapsed into his seat.

Tama turned worried eyes on him briefly, but then picked up where she had left off with taking attendance.

"…"

Letting her voice wash over him, Shido stared silently at the empty desk to his left.

There shouldn't have been any issue. Five years ago, he'd saved Origami's parents when they would have died, and Origami no longer held a grudge against the Spirits. She was probably living quite contentedly somewhere. It was such a happy ending that he was asking to be struck down by divine wrath if he wished for anything more.

For Origami, that original world had been the anomaly. She was meant to live in a kinder world, a girl who was supposed to be raised by loving parents. Yes. It was better like this. This was how the world *should* be.

"Shido?"

Abruptly, he heard Tohka's voice from the desk to his right. It was full of questions and concern.

"Mm." He looked over at her. "What?"

"You…" She leaned toward him. "What's wrong? Does it hurt some place?"

"Huh?" It was only when she said that that he realized tears were streaming down his cheeks and falling on his desk. "Oh…"

He hurried to wipe them away with the sleeve of his uniform. "I'm fine."

Tohka's eyebrows rose into an upside-down V, but maybe she thought it wouldn't be good to push it any further. She didn't say anything else, even though she still looked anxious.

"Why…?" he muttered to himself. *I mean,* crying? Was he happy in the knowledge that Origami was enjoying her life? Or sad he didn't get to see her anymore? He didn't really know himself.

He knew just one thing. Yes. One single thing.

Origami, formerly a prisoner to her desire for vengeance, had been unable to live like a regular girl. The girl who had put herself almost daily onto the battlefield, abandoning both tears and smiles. He wished he could have seen her smile normally, just once.

◇

"…"

Evening. Hair tied back with black ribbons, Kotori stared with hard eyes as she sat facing the wrong way on the sofa in the living room of her own house. Her focus was on the back of her older brother, Shido, at work in the kitchen making supper. The sky-blue apron suited him almost disgustingly well.

This was not an uncommon scene. She couldn't help but feel, however, that he had been off somehow since the morning.

He'd raced down the stairs with incredible energy, checked the date, hugged Kotori, and come at her with a question that made her assume he was still half asleep, and then he came home from school completely changed, with a dull, heavy look on his face. What exactly had happened to make him plummet back to earth like that?

"Hmph." She snorted and flicked the stick of the Chupa Chups in her mouth as she turned around to sit properly on the sofa again. It made her sick. She didn't like that something big enough to shake Shido to the core had happened without her knowing. Grumpily, she recrossed her legs.

"What's…the matter with Shido?" Yoshino asked, in a worried voice, her eyes also on Shido. Fluffy hair, eyes like sapphires. She was about the same height as Kotori, and her small body was currently clad in a pastel-colored dress.

"Right? Seems kinda bummed out." Yoshinon, the rabbit puppet she wore on her left hand, flapped its mouth open and shut.

The girl sitting next to Yoshino, Natsumi, placed a hand on her chin with a bored look (although she was apparently not actually bored at all). "That air of ennui," she said. "It's a woman."

"Wha—?!"

"Huh…?"

Kotori and Yoshino gaped at Natsumi.

"H-hold up," Kotori demanded. "What d'you mean?"

"A…woman?" Yoshino asked doubtfully.

"Oh. Uh." Natsumi immediately looked away like she had lost all confidence in herself. "Maybe I'm wrong. Actually, forget it…"

"No, don't go soft on me now. Spit it out." Kotori grabbed Natsumi's face with both hands and turned it toward her.

The other girl's eyes darted around the room anxiously, but she nodded firmly. "When a teenage boy's moping around, it's basically always a girl."

"So you're saying Shido got dumped by someone?" Kotori pressed her.

"I wouldn't go that far," Natsumi shook her head slightly. "It's just that boys that age, when you get right down to it, basically everything they do is based on what girls are going to think of them. It could be some girls start spreading weird rumors about you, or the girl one seat over gives you the cold shoulder—guys get pretty down with that sort of stuff."

"I-is that how it is…?" Yoshino said, awed.

"Yes," Natsumi asserted. "Also, if you ask her to work on a project with you and she's all 'uhhh' in this kind of I-can't-even-believe-this sort of tone. Or you pick up the eraser she dropped, and she goes, 'Oh… I don't want that anymore. You can have it'…"

"N-Natsumi…?" Kotori raised an anxious eyebrow.

"And when all the clubs are recruiting new members at the start of the year," Natsumi continued, "and you go and apply, and she says, 'Oh! But morning practice is seriously hard. You sure? No, I mean, you don't have to go killing yourself here, y'know?' Or when you're playing dodgeball in gym class, and then I throw the ball, and you scream for real and run away, and I mean, come on! Dammit!" This last part seemed to be her own personal grudge. For a Spirit, she was strangely versed in the challenges of school life.

"G-get ahold of yourself!" Kotori yelled.

"A-anyway. I think it's safe to say something happened at school," Natsumi said, breathing a little heavily.

On that, Kotori was in agreement. She nodded curtly as she glanced at Shido's somehow sad back out of the corner of her eye. "Well, I think we can probably let him be if it's that…"

"But it's hard to watch…Shido being sad," Yoshino said. "Can't we do something…?"

Kotori scratched her head and sighed. "Well, I mean, I'd *like* to do something, but as to how to cheer him up…"

"If a woman can bring a high school boy grief," Natsumi started to say, with a hard glint in her eyes, "then a woman can heal it, too."

Kotori gasped. "A woman? Right, so… Huh?"

"…!"

"Eek! Natsumi's a perv!"

Yoshino and Yoshinon cried out, at last understanding what Natsumi was getting at. Yoshino's cheeks grew red, and Yoshinon covered its face with both hands.

"Hang on a minute." Kotori furrowed her brow and tapped her temples as she flicked the stick of her lollipop up. "Why would I do that for Shido—?"

"I-I'll…do it," Yoshino interrupted her. "If it would make Shido happy again…"

"Yoshino?!" Kotori shrieked in surprise.

"Mm." Natsumi bobbed her head up and down. "Fine. Okay, leave it to me. You'll have him shivering all over, Yoshino. All right, let's do thi—"

"W-wait just a second!" Kotori threw her hands out suddenly.

Natsumi shrank into herself with a shudder.

"I didn't say I *wouldn't* do it," Kotori cried. "I did not say that!"

"Y-yeah." Natsumi stared at her, nervously. "So then, you're in, Kotori?"

"Hmph. I kinda have to be. So?" Kotori asked, crossing her arms. "What exactly is the plan?"

Natsumi held up a finger, as if making a proposal. "Because of all that stuff I was describing to you before, I might be able to use just a bit of Spirit power now."

"Huh?" Kotori said, baffled, her eyes widening. But she quickly realized what Natsumi meant.

Yes. Because of all the Spirits, Natsumi was particularly fragile. Even a small incident like this easily upset her mental state, which could cause some of her Spirit power to flow back into her. And the Spirit Natsumi had the ability to transform her target's appearance.

"Wh-whoa, hold up," Kotori admonished her. "You're not planning to turn us into kids and get that whole 'personal zoo' thing going again, right? You can't do that. Big no. We put Shido into Dad mode, and he'll actually end up even more down in the dumps."

Yes. Natsumi had previously turned Kotori, Yoshino, and the other Spirits into children and dressed them up in animal-print leotards and animal ear headbands.

But Natsumi shook her head back and forth. "We're going with the opposite."

"Huh?"

"The...opposite?"

Kotori and Yoshino looked at each other curiously.

"...! Whoa!" Shido shuddered abruptly while preparing supper. He'd been lost in thought as he chopped up the cabbage, and he'd very nearly cut his finger by accident. "Aah... This is bad. I really need to focus here."

Sighing, he shook his head slightly. He was clearly more concerned about the whole Origami thing than he thought. But he couldn't go on in this mood forever. If he didn't get it together and set his mind properly on cooking, Kotori and the girls would end up feasting on vegetables in blood sauce.

"Woh-kay." He took a deep breath to collect himself and adjusted his grip on the knife.

"Sh-Shido. I'll help."

He heard Kotori's somewhat shaky voice from behind.

"Hmm? Oh, thanks. Then how about you—?" he started to say as he turned around, and then he froze in place. The knife fell from his shaking hand and plunged into the floor.

And that only made sense. Kotori and Yoshino were standing before him, but neither was the young girl Shido thought he knew. Instead, he faced two grown women about the same age as he was. In terms of height, the formerly childish pair were noticeably taller, with that beauty particular to girls on the verge of adulthood. In terms of breast size, Kotori's hadn't changed much at all in contrast to Yoshino's much larger chest.

But this wasn't the only thing that surprised Shido. There was also the matter of their clothes. He didn't know why, but they were both wearing frilly aprons over bathing suits, with little headpieces perched on their heads in the style of summer maids, out of season. Plus they were both clearly embarrassed by how embarrassing this was; their cheeks were red, and they were hunched awkwardly.

"Wh-what are you *wearing*?!" he cried, panicking. "And those bodies—"

The girls looked at each other before stepping up to either side of him clumsily.

"Wh-what does it matter?" Kotori yelped.

"That's...right," Yoshino agreed. "Anyway, please...let us help."

"H-help?" Shido broke out in a sweat. Because the girls had tangled themselves around each of his arms, a single careless move threatened to bring him into contact with their chests. Yoshino was especially dangerous. He seemed to have a little more leeway with Kotori.

"Shido?" Kotori fixed a glare on him, like she had intuited exactly what was going on in his mind. "Are you maybe thinking something extremely rude?"

"...!" He hurriedly shook his head. Now that he was thinking about it, Kaguya had said something similar that very morning. He very nearly asked if a smaller chest gave a girl a sharper intuition, but if he dared to blurt anything like that, he was liable to end up finely sliced and served for supper, so he refrained.

The situation was so strange, he almost wondered if he was

dreaming. But he wasn't entirely clueless about how this was happening. And that only made sense. Because, in his own subjective time, he had only yesterday been the benefactor of this power.

"Natsumi!" he cried. "This is your doing, isn't it?!" He saw the girl peeking out from behind the sofa shudder.

After a moment of silence, she slowly poked her face up, like she had resigned herself to her fate. This was, of course, the Spirit of transformation, Natsumi.

Just like Kotori and Yoshino, Natsumi had matured into a teenager. But she was wearing a regular maid's uniform, rather than the provocative outfits the other girls had on.

"Hey! Whoa! What the—?" Kotori shouted upon seeing her. "Natsumi! Why are you not in a swimsuit?! We all agreed to go with the swimsuit, didn't we?!"

"Oh." Natsumi averted her eyes awkwardly. "It's just, you know... when I thought about it, it was too embarrassing, like I'd feel, you know, stupid..."

"But you were okay with *us* looking stupid?!"

"K-Kotori... Calm down..." Yoshino tried to pacify her, but Kotori was apparently not done. She rolled up imaginary sleeves and lunged for Natsumi.

"I'll put you in this stupid outfit myself!"

"Eeaaah!" Natsumi shrieked and fled from her place behind the sofa.

Kotori was determined, however. As the two girls raced around the living room, she yelled, "You stop right there! I'll rip those clothes off you!"

"Noooo!" Natsumi cried, tears in her eyes. "I'm! Being! Ravished!"

"No one is ravishing anybody!" Kotori shouted. They stomped around in circles, causing dust to dance into the air.

"H-hey, both of you! Settle down!" Shido yelled, trying to stop the girls as he wiped his hands on his apron and marched into the living room.

Yoshino trailed after him, a troubled look on her face. "Fighting... is bad..."

But this act only led to failure. Because the chase was happening in the living room, with its many obstacles, Natsumi tripped on a bump in the carpet and fell toward Shido and Yoshino. Naturally, being hot on her heels, Kotori wasn't able to stop when she fell. She dived head-first toward Natsumi's back.

"Ah! Gah!"

"Wha—?!"

"Eek...!"

"Hey—!"

Four voices mixed together, and then the table and the sofa were dragged into the whole mess, and there was a magnificent crash. The cloud of dust from Kotori and Natsumi's chase looked paltry in comparison to the new mess.

"Ow-ow-ow... Is everyone o...kay?!" Shido righted himself with a groan, his voice sliding up into a shriek.

When they fell, his face had ended up inside Natsumi's skirt. His field of view was filled with Natsumi's bottom, the bare skin of which was separated from him by a flimsy bit of cloth.

"Eeeaaaah!"

"Wh-whaaaaa?!"

Natsumi and Shido shouted at the same time, and Natsumi leaped to her feet as if propelled away by an invisible force. And squashed Shido's face momentarily.

"Hey! What are you doing, Shido?!" Kotori demanded.

"A-are you all right, Shido...?" Yoshino sounded concerned.

"Y-yeah—" He started to answer them and then cut himself off. The girls must have gotten caught on something when they fell—Kotori's bikini bottoms had slid down, and Yoshino's bra top had come undone. He caught a glimpse of her full bosom peeking out from the sides of the apron. (Yoshinon had saved the day with a good catch.)

A heartbeat later, the girls themselves noticed the issue. They dropped their eyes on their own bodies, and their faces turned red.

""Eeeeeaaaaah?!"" they shrieked in unison, crouching in an attempt to cover up.

Natsumi was pushed backward by their momentum, and her bottom dropped onto Shido's face once again.

"Eeeeaaah!!"

"…?!"

Three screams and one soundless shout echoed through the Itsuka living room.

"Haaaaah." Shido let out a long sigh as he pressed a cold, wet towel to the end of his nose a few minutes later. "You're killing me here."

Kotori, Yoshino, and Natsumi had returned to their original forms, and their small shoulders slumped apologetically as they saw the shape Shido was in.

"Hmph. Our bad."

"I'm sorry…Shido."

"Sorry."

They apologized in turn, starting with Kotori on the right.

After sighing once more, Shido gave them a weary smile. "It's okay. Forget it. Sorry I made you worry about me. You were trying to cheer me up, right?"

The three girls nodded, still hanging their heads.

Shido scratched his cheek thoughtfully. Apparently, he'd been so obviously depressed that they had easily picked up on it. He'd been told on a daily basis to be careful that he didn't upset the mental state of the Spirits, and now here he was doing basically the opposite. He set the towel down on the table and pulled his face into a smile for them.

"Thanks," he said. "I'm all good now. No worries." He could see them visibly relax at this.

Kotori's eyes flew open in surprise, and then she crossed her arms like she was trying to play tough. "H-hmph. Well, fine then. I'm not going to interrogate you about what happened or anything, but if you keep moping like that, you'll make the Spirits anxious."

"Yeah. I said I was sorry." Shido shrugged and his smile grew wider. He found Kotori's act more adorable than anything else.

But Kotori herself apparently did not love being condescended to by him. Her mouth pulled downward into a frown, and she continued. "I need you to be focused. You never know when another Spirit's going to appear. Could be an unknown Spirit, of course, and there's also Kurumi. Plus we've got Devil—"

"Huh?" He automatically furrowed his brow at this code name. Devil. This was a name he'd never heard. "H-hang on a second, Kotori. 'Devil'…? Which Spirit's that?"

But now it was Kotori's turn to frown dubiously. "What are you talking about, Shido? You know, Devil? The Spirit hunter? The Spirit we need to be most on guard against? Her and 'Nightmare' Kurumi Tokisaki. Don't tell me you forgot who she is."

"Her and Kurumi?" Beads of sweat gathered on his forehead.

This world had moved in a slightly different direction from the world he knew. This day had beaten that knowledge quite thoroughly into him. So it was entirely possible that a Spirit he didn't know had made her grand entrance on the scene. But he couldn't grasp right away that this new Spirit warranted as much caution as the very worst of the Spirits, Kurumi.

Kotori crossed her arms, looking even more dubious. "Are you being serious? What is up with you today exactly? It's like everything before yesterday got knocked right out of your head."

"…Oh, sorry." He bowed apologetically. She was pretty close to hitting the mark, actually.

She sighed heavily again and flicked up the stick of the Chupa Chups in her mouth. "So you *really* don't remember?"

"U-uhh," he stammered. "Maybe you could just explain this Devil to me?"

Kotori sighed again. "Devil. Although we've confirmed manifestation in this world, she's a totally unknown Spirit. We've had no success in making contact. And." She paused a beat before continuing. "This is just a maybe, but she's inverted."

"Wha…?!" His eyes flew open. "Inverted…? Meaning? Are you saying an inverted Spirit can just appear like normal?"

"I *told* you, we don't know the specifics," she said, annoyed. This was no doubt information that the Shido of this world had long been aware of.

Why would an inverted Spirit appear? He had no answer to this, but there were still a number of other things he didn't understand. He shook his head and continued questioning her.

"What about this Spirit-hunting you mentioned?" he asked.

"Means just what it sounds like." She shrugged. "Devil doesn't appear alone. She always shows up when another Spirit manifests... and she attacks that Spirit. I mean, Natsumi here would've been in real trouble if Tohka and them hadn't shown up to help." She looked toward Natsumi.

Perhaps remembering this time, Natsumi shuddered slightly.

"H-hang on a second." He frowned. "She attacks *Spirits*?"

"Yes." Kotori nodded firmly. "Almost like the AST or DEM. At first, we suspected one of those organizations was involved. Like, what if they'd tamed a Spirit and made it hunt other Spirits... But as far as we can tell, Devil doesn't have a cooperative relationship with the AST or DEM. Both groups have actually attacked her."

"So then...why would Devil...?" He trailed off.

"No idea." She shrugged with exaggeration. "She probably has her reasons, but we can't know unless we actually ask her. And she always flashes off somewhere right away, so Ratatoskr still hasn't made contact."

Shido put a hand to his chin while a bead of sweat trailed down his cheek.

Devil, a Spirit who hunted Spirits. He felt a curious sense of wrongness bloom in his heart upon hearing this name.

"Hey? Can I see a video or picture of this Devil?" he asked.

"We've got that, but...I don't think you'll get much from it?"

"Huh?" He frowned. "What do you mean?"

"Well." Kotori scratched her head, groaning as she flicked the stick of her lollipop up and down. "I guess a picture's worth a thousand words. Hang on just a sec."

She got up and left the living room. She returned soon enough, carrying a terminal the size of a piece of paper.

"Here. Take a look." She set the device on the table and pressed PLAY.

The video of an utterly destroyed city. Explosions and smoke filled the air, communicating the fact that a battle was in progress that very second.

And in the midst of all this, he saw it. A human silhouette clad in darkness. So this was what Kotori meant. At best, he could just barely make out that there was someone on-screen, their face shrouded in darkness. But numerous feathery parts floating around this human shape persuasively told the story of why it had been named "Devil."

"Ah," he said quietly. Not because of the unusual appearance of this Spirit. But because he had seen this Spirit before. He really couldn't see her face or make out any expression on it. But he knew. He had been face-to-face with this Spirit before.

"No…way…" His teeth began to chatter. His whole body shook. Because this was… "Ori…gami…"

It was indeed the inverted Spirit, Origami.

The next day, Shido went to school with Tohka, just like the day before. He yawned long and loudly as he sat down at his desk.

In the seat to his right, Tohka widened her eyes curiously. "Mm. You sleepy, Shido?"

"Yeah." He nodded. "I couldn't really sleep last night."

"Mm. That's no good. You okay?"

"Ha-ha, well… I'll take a nap once school's over, before supper." He grinned and then wiped away the tears that popped into his eyes before sighing and looking absently at the desk to his left. The desk where Origami would have been in his original world.

"…"

He was all too aware of the cause of his sleeplessness. Last night, he had done two things. The first was to go out. After supper, he'd slipped out of the house alone and headed to a couple particular locations—the apartment building where Origami had lived in his original world and the residential district of Nanko, where the fire had been five years earlier.

He went for one reason and one reason alone: He thought that Origami might have been there. But reality was not so kind as that.

No one was living in the apartment, and the house where the Tobiichis had lived had a different nameplate at the gate now. He'd asked the family that currently lived there about the Tobiichis, but they didn't know their whereabouts.

"Origami," he said to no one in particular as he looked at the seat with no one in it.

The video that Kotori had shown him the day before. The mysterious Spirit, Devil, had without a doubt been Origami Tobiichi. And she hadn't been any ordinary Spirit; she was inverted.

He gritted his teeth. He didn't get it.

In that past world of five years ago, he had supposedly succeeded in changing history. Origami should have been able to live in a normal world as a normal girl. And yet… How exactly had she become a Spirit? And why had she inverted?

Plus, she was attacking other Spirits, according to Kotori. In which case, nothing had changed from when she was with the AST, had it? And when the Spirit was Lost, Devil also vanished in the blink of an eye. It was thanks to this that the city managed to get by without too much damage when she appeared.

He didn't understand any of it; his head was swimming. What exactly had happened to this world in those five years? Shido scratched his head.

"Dammit! Why this of all things…?" he said, annoyed, as he recalled the other action he had taken the day before.

That had been to gather as much information as possible on this world. The moment he learned about this world's Origami, he'd been consumed by fathomless anxiety and doubt. What if something else, different from his memories, had also happened in this world and he just didn't know about it? Or maybe something that should have happened hadn't? He couldn't stop thinking this.

He talked to Kotori when he got home, and (although she looked at him with extreme suspicion) he had gotten a peek at the *Fraxinus* database. As a result, he had learned that history in this world had unfolded more or less as it had in his memory.

Five years earlier, Kotori had become a Spirit and was discovered by Ratatoskr. On April 10, Shido met Tohka and sealed her powers. After that, he sealed Yoshino, met Kurumi and Mana, sealed the Yamai sisters, crossed swords with DEM, sealed Miku and Natsumi. All of it had happened just the way he knew it had.

Yes. Neatly excepting anything to do with Origami Tobiichi.

And while he was thinking about this, the bell rang, the door to the classroom opened, and his homeroom teacher Tama entered. Following the shouted commands of the class rep, he stood, bowed, and took his seat once more.

"Okay. Good morning, everyone. Let's do our best today!" Tama said, smiling.

But Shido barely heard her. Holding his chin in his hands, elbows propped on his desk, he stared absently out the window.

"…"

He really had to talk to Origami at least once. This was the conclusion he'd arrived at after spending the night thinking.

When he had learned the day before that no one knew her, that *he* hadn't even met Origami in this world, he'd thought that he would never have anything to do with her. He'd actually believed this could be a good thing for her. He'd felt like he couldn't go butting into her new happy life. He'd thought that was all fine and good when he'd assumed that she was off somewhere in the world living quietly.

But now that he had seen that video, he could no longer be comfortable in that assumption. The ravages of war still surrounded Origami. His mission wasn't over yet. The inconstant world was still placing the cruel burden of destiny on this girl's shoulders.

That said, however, the Shido of this moment knew far too little about this world. He realized he wouldn't get anywhere unless he met and talked with Origami.

But there were several walls between him and that goal. For starters, the Origami of this world didn't know him. And more importantly, he didn't even know where exactly she was.

"I'm really not going to get anywhere by myself," he said, too quietly for anyone else to hear, tapping a fingertip on his desk. If he was going to make a move, he'd need Ratatoskr's help. His only choice maybe was to explain the situation to Kotori when he got home that day and get her to help him look for Origami. He had his doubts as to whether or not she'd believe that he'd traveled through time and changed the world, but he was sure she wouldn't dismiss him out of hand if it was about the Spirit Devil.

"Woh-kay..." Looking out the window, Shido clenched his hands into fists, as if to firm up his resolve.

"Oh, right," Tama said at the same time, like she'd only just remembered. "I want to introduce you all to a new friend. Please come in!"

The classroom door rattled open, and a girl stepped inside. A transfer student, apparently.

He thought it was weird to have a transfer student at this time of year, but he had bigger fish to fry right now. He didn't bother to turn his whole head in the direction of the new student, just his eyes.

"Huh?" Those eyes grew wide in amazement at seeing the girl who walked up to the teacher's podium.

A girl with a delicate figure and a graceful, doll-like face. The hair that hung down her back was pale, making her look like a princess from a foreign country.

He could feel his classmates' excitement the moment she appeared. The boys leaned forward with gasps, and the girls also lit up with curiosity.

He alone was dumbfounded as he stared at her face. The reason was simple. He had seen her before.

"All right. If you would please introduce yourself?" Tama urged the transfer student.

The girl nodded neatly, turned to face the class, and said in a quiet voice, "I'm Origami Tobiichi. It's nice to meet all of you." She bowed deeply.

Everyone else in class started whispering excitedly. Some of them remembered that Shido had uttered the unusual name "Origami" only the day before. They cocked their heads curiously to one side, and perhaps reading something vulgar into the coincidence, turned mischievous smiles on Shido.

But he didn't have the extra brain space to deal with this at the moment.

"Wha…?" His voice shook, and his eyes were wide as dinner plates.

Although her hair was a different length, this was without a doubt the very same Origami Tobiichi he remembered.

While he was too stunned to speak, Tama let her eyes roam over the classroom.

"Let's see. Okay, Tobiichi, your desk is…" She paused, and then pointed in his direction. "The seat next to Itsuka is empty. Would you please take a seat there?"

"Yes, of course," Origami agreed and walked leisurely toward Shido. But after she had taken a few steps, she stopped abruptly.

He quickly understood why. Their eyes had met because he was staring at her.

"Oh!" Her eyes widened in surprise.

"Huh…?" At the same time, a short cry escaped his own throat.

She had met the eyes of a boy seriously scrutinizing her. He could understand that kind of surprise. But for some reason, he felt like that wasn't what had shocked her.

"No way. You…," she said, almost as though she recognized him from somewhere. But she quickly shook her head as if to get her mind back on track. She turned and bowed in a reserved manner before settling into the seat Tama had directed her to.

"…"

Watching Origami carry out this series of actions, Shido felt his heart start pounding faster. What *was* that? Did she *know* him? When he thought about it, there was no way. But then why did she…?

"Okay! Let's get back to attendance!" Tama began to call out names again in a cheery voice, but Shido didn't register a word of it.

Chapter 9
Instinct

"...Wha—?" Kotori's voice over the phone was incredulous.

But that was no wonder. If she had called him out of the blue during a break at school and told him *that,* Shido no doubt would have had a similar reaction.

Yes. Once homeroom was over, he'd slipped from the classroom, found a spot where he could be alone, and called Kotori. At first, she had listened absently, saying a word every now and again to show that she was still there, but then he heard the rustle of what sounded like hair ribbons being switched, and she uttered the earlier question.

"Hold up," she said, sounding bewildered. *"Exactly* what *are you talking about? Give me the deets."*

"It's just like I said. Devil transferred into my class," he told her.

"And I'm telling you I don't get it. Why on earth would Devil go to school, of all places?" She sounded like she was snarling. *"And like, more importantly, we don't know who Devil is. We haven't been able to get a name or even a look at her face. How do you know for sure this transfer student is Devil?"*

"Oh, uh...," Shido stammered. It was a perfectly reasonable question. "I don't have time right now. I'll explain everything when I get home. But it's true. You have to believe me."

"..." Kotori was silent for a second or two before finally letting out

a sigh. *"Fine. I'll send a measurement device over. What we do next depends on the results we get there. You got no problems with that, yeah?"*

"…! So you believe me?!" he cried out in surprise. He'd been the one to bring this to her, but her words were still a little unexpected.

"To be honest, I'm only halfway there," she replied, sounding exasperated. *"But if someone comes and tells me they know who Devil really is when I got nothing on her, well, I can't exactly sit on that."* She paused briefly. *"And I can't imagine you'd call to tell me something like that without good reason. No… Actually, even if it's just a hunch at this point, you've done enough to convince me."*

"Kotori…"

"But if this turns out to be some convoluted scheme to get Ratatoskr to check out some girl you're kinda into, I'll make you pay."

"I—I would never!" he cried.

"Mm," Kotori assented. *"I'll have her checked out right away. Umm, what was her name again?"*

"Origami," he said. "Origami Tobiichi."

"Origami Tobiichi? Tobiichi…" She stopped short and then continued, as if she'd just remembered something. *"Wait. You mean, the AST's Origami Tobiichi?"*

"Huh?!" he yelped in surprise.

The AST. Short for the Anti-Spirit Team within the Self-Defense Forces. Origami had indeed belonged to this organization. But that was supposed to have been in his original world. There was no way for Kotori to have known that.

He gasped. "Kotori, you don't actually have memories of the original world, do you?"

"Uh? What are you talking about? You still dreaming like yesterday?" Kotori replied coolly. *"If I remember right, there was someone who went by that name in the AST. Fought Tohka and them a million times. But she retired a little while ago."*

"Wha—?" He was at a loss for words. It wasn't that Kotori had remembered events from the original world. That meant the new-world Origami was once in the AST as well.

"Why on earth…?" he muttered.

"Why did she quit, you mean?" Kotori said with a snort, misinterpreting Shido's question to himself. *"That I don't know. But now that you mention it, Origami Tobiichi quit the AST right around the time Devil started showing up. Hmm. If the reason she left was that she had been turned into a Spirit…"* She trailed off, lost in thought.

But half of what she was saying went in one ear and out the other for him. Shido's head was still spinning at the fact that Origami had been in the AST.

She'd joined this group in the original world because she wanted to take down the Spirit who had killed her parents. What could have compelled her to join up in this world, where her parents had been saved?

"*Hey, Shido,*" Kotori barked. "*You listening to me?*"

"…! Y-yeah… Sorry." Shido came back to himself.

"Honestly." He could almost hear her rolling her eyes. *"Get it together. At any rate, we'll look into whether Origami Tobiichi's a Spirit or not. Report back to me on anything else you notice. But if this Origami Tobiichi really is Devil, then she's an extremely dangerous inversion. Don't go doing anything reckless."*

"R-right. Got it," he said, hanging up.

"…"

He shoved his phone into his pocket and leaned back against the wall. Too many bits of information were entangled in his head, and he couldn't sort it all out. But he'd get nowhere standing here like this. He took a deep breath and returned to Grade 11, Class 4.

When he stepped inside, he found a crowd around the window seat. Apparently, everyone was deeply interested in the cute transfer student. Origami herself wore a baffled look on her face in the center of this cluster of his classmates.

At exactly that moment, the bell rang to signal the start of class, and they all waved at her and returned to their seats. He watched as she waved back and then sighed.

"Ha-ha." His face automatically relaxed into a smile at this unfamiliar sight. He'd never seen a hint of an expression on the face of the Origami he'd known.

Which made him wonder all over again. Why had Origami joined the AST in this world, too? Why had she become a Spirit? Why had she inverted? And why, despite the fact that she'd inverted, was she in possession of her own mind and able to return to human form like this? The more he thought about it, the more questions he had.

While he let his thoughts race, the teacher entered the classroom. "Class has started. Sit down!"

"Oh… Sorry." Shido hurriedly sat down at his desk and pulled out his books. But perhaps it was obvious that he wouldn't be able to focus on the lesson. He kept glancing at Origami. He really did need to at least talk to her. He didn't know anything about the Origami of this world.

But when the break came, the cluster of people returned. He wasn't going to get his chance to chat with her if this kept up.

"…"

After thinking it over for a bit, he scribbled something on a page from his notebook, folded it up, and slipped it onto Origami's desk when the teacher wasn't looking.

"…?" Origami cocked her head slightly to one side when she saw it. She reached out to unfold the scrap of paper and looked at the text written on it. Her eyes grew round in surprise.

At lunch that day, Shido slipped from the classroom and went to the stairs leading up to the roof. Because it was separated from the block where the classrooms were, almost no students ventured near this area. In fact, the stairway was steeped in solitude, as if it existed in an alternate reality disconnected from the tumult of students echoing throughout the rest of the school.

But that didn't mean he was entirely alone.

A girl was already standing there waiting. The transfer student who was all anyone could talk about, Origami Tobiichi.

There were likely students who spent all three years of their high school career oblivious to the fact that a remote place like this existed. Normally, it would be strange for a transfer student, of all people, to be there.

But Shido wasn't surprised. Because…

"Um. Here." Origami pulled a piece of notebook paper from her pocket and showed it to him. On it was a message to the effect that she should come here at lunch, written in his own hand.

Yes. Shido was the one who'd asked Origami to come.

"Hey," he said. "Sorry for making you come all the way out here."

"Mm-hmm. That's fine, but…what did you need?" she asked, her face tensing slightly.

But of course, that only made sense. She had been asked to come to this deserted place by a male student she'd only just met. It made sense that she was a little on edge, like she was maybe in danger. In fact, he was almost grateful that she had come here alone, as he'd requested.

But somehow, the experience of her being on guard against him, rather than of him being on guard against her, was a novel one.

"Oh…" He scratched his cheek, uncertain of exactly where to start. He had a million questions for her, but it was possible that she would only become more guarded if he abruptly began to interrogate her. And then he remembered what she'd said that morning. "So, uh, Origami?"

"Huh?" she said, jerking her head up.

For a moment, he couldn't understand why that would shock her, but then he got it. "S-sorry… Tobiichi. I shouldn't have said that. It's rude to call you by your first name out of the blue."

"Mm-hmm. I just didn't expect it," she said with a slight shake of her head. "Umm…Itsuka."

He smiled wryly at the unfamiliar sound of his last name in her mouth.

"Is something the matter?" she asked.

"Oh, no. Nothing," he replied. "Anyway, Tobiichi. This morning, when you saw my face, you said something, right? What was that about?"

"Ohh…" Her gaze grew slightly vacant, like she was going back in her memory. "I'm sorry if I upset you, Itsuka. I just had a bit of a shock when I saw you, because you look exactly like someone I met a long time ago."

"Huh?" He frowned unconsciously. "Was it…me?"

"Mm-hmm. It couldn't have been. I mean, I met him five years ago. You would've still been in elementary school. And…" She abruptly lowered her eyes. "He's dead. He died five years ago, in front of me."

"…!" Hearing this, he realized the true identity of the person she was talking about. It was without a doubt Shido himself. When he'd saved her parents that day, he had met Origami's eyes for the most fleeting of instances.

"Is that all you wanted? I'm going back to the classroom." She turned to go down the stairs.

"…! Oh! Wait just a second." He hurried to stop her. He still hadn't gotten any of the information he wanted. He couldn't see himself making any real progress playing the ignorant student, though. He took a deep breath and opened his mouth. "This person you met five years ago, was it maybe during the big fire in the Nanko district?"

"Huh? How did you…?" she started to say with wide eyes, and then she gasped. "Was it…? Was that your older brother, Itsuka?"

"Uh?" he squeaked idiotically. So she thought the person she'd met that day was his older brother. But anyone would make that same assumption. She'd never believe him if he said it had been him.

He didn't love letting the misunderstanding stand, but he didn't really have much of a choice if it meant that the conversation would proceed smoothly.

"Well… Something like that," Shido said, and the look on Origami's face immediately changed. Her eyebrows came together, and she looked like she would burst into tears at any second. "T-Tobiichi…?"

"…!"

She stepped toward him, took his hand, and bowed deeply. "Your brother saved my mother and father. If he hadn't been there, they would have both died. I may never be able to thank you enough, but please let me say this. Thank you…truly!"

"Uh-huh…," he replied vaguely, stunned by her reaction. But her words brought him a key piece of information. He had indeed succeeded in saving her parents five years earlier. He let out a short sigh of relief.

"Oh!" She gasped, released his hand, and bowed again, her cheeks flushing a deep red. "I-I'm sorry. Out of the blue like that."

"No. It's okay." He smiled faintly, feeling a curious sensation at this un-Origami-like behavior. But at the same time as that one fact became clear, another mystery deepened. "Umm, so your parents were okay then, right?"

"Yes." She nodded.

He held his breath for a second before continuing. "So then you all live together?"

"No," she said, lowering her eyes. "My parents were killed in a traffic accident four years ago."

"...?! What...?!" Shido couldn't help but cry out. "B-but..."

The phrase "history's power to correct itself" flitted through his mind. Kurumi had neither confirmed nor denied it, but a sense of helplessness overcame him, the idea that no matter what he did, in the end, he couldn't change the conclusion of Origami's parents dying. He shuddered in fear.

"Itsuka...?" Origami frowned dubiously. And of course she did. It was only natural that she would think it weird for a boy she'd just met that very day to have this kind of outsize reaction. But then she shook her head, as if quickly rethinking things, and bowed her head. "I'm sorry. After your brother sacrificed himself to save them."

"No, I mean—," he started to say.

"But." Origami interrupted as she raised her face and continued with a severe look. "In that year they were alive after your brother saved them, my parents gave me so, so much. That time together is priceless, and I never would have had it if your brother hadn't given up everything. I really am grateful."

He could see no sign of a lie on the face of Origami as she said this.

"Y-yeah?" he replied, averting his eyes slightly. It was too bad that Origami's parents were dead, and he felt sorry for her. But hearing her speak now really lifted his spirits. He felt like all his efforts hadn't been for nothing.

But she'd said that the cause of her parents' death was a traffic accident. If that was true, then...

He lifted his face and stared into her eyes as he swallowed hard, made up his mind, and opened his mouth. "So then...why did you join the AST, Origami?"

"What—?" She gasped.

Yes. This was Shido's question. On the day of the fire, Origami's parents had escaped the Angel's blow. In which case, Origami shouldn't have hated the Spirits. So then why?

"How do you know—?" she said, and then furrowed her brow like she was remembering something. She looked at him suspiciously. "You haven't actually gone outside during a spacequake alarm, have you, Itsuka?"

"Huh? O-oh," he stammered.

Right. It was possible that when she was a member of the AST, the Origami of this world had also seen Shido racing toward the epicenter to talk with the Spirit. There was no point in lying to her here.

"Y-yeah," he confessed. "Actually."

"I *knew* it," she said. "I wasn't seeing things."

"Huh?" He frowned. He hadn't expected this response.

"I brought it up with the squad countless times," she continued. "That there was a civilian in the danger zone. I thought it looked like *him*, but to think it was actually you, Itsuka." Her gaze grew stern. "It's extremely dangerous. Please refrain from staying outside in the future."

"Uh. Umm," he responded vaguely, pressed for a response. She could say that all she wanted, but as long as he had his mission with Ratatoskr, he would have to keep going out to stand before the Spirits. He braced himself for her to follow up further, but she didn't try to dig into the situation any deeper.

Instead, she got a firm and determined look on her face as she stared back at him. "The reason I joined the AST...was it?"

"Yeah." He nodded. "If you don't mind telling me?"

"Itsuka." She leaned forward slightly. "The fact that you know about the AST means you also know the cause of the spacequakes?"

He hesitated and then said "Spirits."

"That's right. A uniquely catastrophic creature, the Spirit. And you may have already looked into this, but during that fire five years ago, it was a Spirit who killed your brother."

"I—I...," he stammered. He was here, still very much alive, but in the moment that bolt of light had hit the ground, it could have only looked to her like a person's reality shattering before her very eyes.

She clenched her hands into tight fists as she continued. "He sacrificed himself to save my parents. It's thanks to him that I'm here now. Which is why I started thinking that I didn't want anyone else to end up like that. I decided to become a person who could protect people from the Spirits."

"Oh." He heard himself say this unintentionally. He felt the scattered puzzle pieces snap together in his head.

The Origami in the original world vowed to defeat the Spirits because of her rage over the murder of her parents at the hand of a Spirit. To prevent her from harboring this grudge, Shido had gone back to the world of five years earlier and succeeded in saving her parents. But the secondary event of his "death" when her parents survived had become the new spark that ignited Origami's resolve. It was...ironic. Shido felt his heart stir at this cruel joke of fate.

"...Itsuka?" Origami cocked her head curiously to one side, perhaps wondering at his sudden silence.

"Oh." His fingertips trembled slightly. "Uh, it's nothing..." It was actually a whole lot more than nothing, but he couldn't say anything else in the moment.

He had succeeded in changing the world. But Origami had still witnessed the Spirit killing someone in the end. But this didn't mean all hope was lost. The things that had happened in the original world and this world were different. At first glance, it looked as though the results had been the same, but in the original world, it had been her parents who were killed, people she'd spent her whole life with, while in contrast with that, in this world, she had seen the death of a boy whose name she hadn't even known. And above all else, that boy was alive and well, right here and now. If he could just manage to explain this to her or...

However. He bit his lip. He'd forgotten one important detail—the

Origami of this world had not only been turned into a Spirit, she was also inverted.

Shido didn't really know the ins and outs of this inversion thing. But one thing he did know was that it occurred when the Spirit was plunged into despair.

"…"

He looked at Origami once more. Her tone and the air about her were indeed different from the Origami he knew. But at the very least, the girl before him now didn't appear to have lost hope in this world or to be drowning in misery.

Kotori had clearly instructed him not to do anything reckless. But he couldn't *not* ask her.

"Can I ask one more thing?"

"What is it?" She tilted her head to one side.

He took a deep breath and then gave voice to his question. "Why did you become…a Spirit?"

However.

"Sorry?" She only stared at him, uncomprehending. "Er, become a Spirit? What do you mean?"

"Huh?" Now it was his turn to stare in confusion. For a second, he thought she was feigning innocence, but no. She appeared to honestly have no idea what he was talking about.

"How can that be? I'm sure that was…," he muttered to himself. Just as he set his mind to work, the first bell echoed throughout the school. It seemed that lunch break was already over.

"Looks like lunch is over. I'll go on ahead. Thank you, Itsuka. I'm really glad we got to have this talk," she said, starting down the stairs.

"Ah…," he half groaned, as if to cling to her receding back. There were still so many things he didn't know. He got the feeling that he couldn't let her leave now. "C-can we talk a little more?"

"But class is about to start?" she protested.

"It doesn't have to be today! One day when you're free, can we do this again?"

"Huh? Are you—?" Origami looked shocked and then flushed red.

Shido understood this reaction a heartbeat later, and his own face turned red. "Ah."

The way I said that, it totally sounded like I was asking her on a date!

"U-umm," he stammered, unsure of how to correct this, and Origami averted her eyes.

"Um," she said finally. "Can I have a little time to think about it?"

"Huh? O-of course!" he replied reflexively, and she bowed quickly.

"All right. I'll see you in class!" She practically flew down the stairs.

"…"

To be honest, it was an unexpected sight. If he remarked on how girlish she was, that would have been somewhat rude to the Origami of his original world, but either way, her reaction was very unusual for Origami.

"Aah." He slowly shook his head. Origami had no doubt originally been this sort of girl. Her personality had changed into something rational and cold, due to the death of her parents.

But it was strange. While he did think this Origami was adorable, he felt a strange sadness or a kind of absence somewhere in his heart.

"Guess I was a little too used to the old Origami," he said self-deprecatingly, and followed her down the stairs.

Muttering lifelessly to himself, he went down the hallway and returned to the classroom of Grade 11, Class 4. The English teacher was not far behind him, and fifth period began soon after he sat down at his desk.

At some point during the class, he caught Origami from the corner of his eye, sitting at the desk to his left and suddenly moving oddly.

"Hmm?" He turned his gaze in her direction and saw that she was writing in neat characters on a page ripped from her notebook. And then she folded this in half and set it on his desk when the teacher wasn't looking. Just like he had done during first period.

"Huh…?" He picked it up and started to unfold it.

"…!" Origami's cheeks turned bright red, and her eyes darted about restlessly before she propped her textbook up and hid her face behind it.

◇

"..."

After school that day, Shido went up to the roof by himself, lay on the ground, and stared absently at the clouds drifting by. He pulled out the piece of paper folded in half in his pocket and held it up to the sky.

"I'm free this Saturday."

This was the note he had gotten from Origami earlier. The answer to his invitation, apparently. Below this message was an e-mail address in small letters.

"Saturday..." He folded the page back up and stretched lightly.

He'd managed to get her to meet him, at any rate. Considering the fact that this was a girl he'd only just met (more or less) and that he'd done it without Ratatoskr's help, it was no exaggeration to say this was a spectacular victory for him. That said, however, he still had a whole heap of other issues to sort out.

To start with, was it really possible for Origami to be a Spirit, and inverted at that, and yet to have absolutely no awareness of it?

A number of potential explanations came to mind. The stupidest, but also most likely, was that he had gotten the wrong idea. It had definitely looked like Origami in the video Kotori had shown him. But he couldn't definitively say there was absolutely no other Spirit with an Astral Dress like Origami's.

It was also possible that Origami had straight up lied to him. That wasn't the impression he got, but it wasn't as if he were a criminal psychologist or a master poker player. It didn't require much imagination to think of a scenario where he had been duped by a performance.

Or...

"There can't actually be...*two* Origamis...right?" he said with an empty laugh.

Whatever it was, he'd have to discuss this with Ratatoskr, too.

He was thinking about getting up when an enormous yawn escaped him. At the same time, the strength gradually drained from his body.

But of course, this only made sense. He'd been digging through the database all night, so he hadn't really been able to sleep much.

"Ori…gami…" Murmuring her name, Shido slowly closed his eyes.

After some unknown period of time, he let out a little groan and opened his eyes again. "Ngh…"

A few seconds later, as his brain woke up, he realized that he must have fallen asleep at some point. He was apparently more exhausted than he'd thought.

"Ah." He sighed. "Not good. What time is it?"

He moved to pull his phone from his pocket to check the time, and then frowned at the feeling that something was off.

"Hmm?" Something was different from before he fell asleep. After mulling it over for a few moments, he realized what it was. A pillow. There hadn't been anything beneath his head before, but now he felt a strangely soft sensation there.

When he reached a hand up to find out what this pillow was, a girl's face popped into his field of view.

"Oh dear me," she cooed. "Don't you go getting up to any mischief here."

"Gah?!" His eyes flew open, adrenaline flooding his veins.

A heartbeat later, Shido realized that the soft sensation beneath his head was this girl's legs.

"K-Kurumi?!" He shrieked her name.

Yes. The girl who had popped into his field of view was the Spirit who'd sent him back to the past, Kurumi Tokisaki. Apparently, his head had ended up on her lap at some point.

"Hee-hee-hee!" she giggled. "Good day to you, Shido. You looked quite adorable while asleep."

"…!" He was exceedingly embarrassed and bolted from her folded knees beneath his head.

"Oh goodness!" She smiled, as though she found Shido's reaction amusing, and stood up gracefully. Instead of her familiar red-and-black Astral Dress, she was in the Raizen High School uniform she'd

had on when he'd first met her. Her left eye and the clockface etched into it were hidden by her long bangs.

"Kurumi, you…" Shido braced himself.

Now that he thought about it, it wasn't necessarily the case that the Kurumi who existed in this world would have the same memories as the Kurumi he knew. That was a hard lesson that he'd learned that day. He obviously had to be on guard against her, the very worst of the Spirits.

But her eyes grew round at his reaction, and then she put a hand to her mouth and began to laugh. "You needn't be so vigilant against me, Shido. If I had intended to *eat* you, I would've helped myself while you were helplessly asleep."

"Unh…" He felt a bead of sweat roll down his cheek. She was exactly right. But that still didn't mean she was someone he could relax around. Even as he nodded his agreement with what she said, he kept a sharp eye on her movements.

"Oh my, my! You *are* a suspicious one, hmm? And here I thought we were partners who changed the world together." She shrugged playfully.

At this, Shido's eyes flew open, and he gasped. "Kurumi, you—"

"Yes, I remember," she told him. "The original world. Origami."

"…!" He felt all the hair on his body stand on end. That was only natural. Because for the first time since coming to this world, he had encountered someone other than himself who knew about Origami. It was like a traveler dropped in the middle of the desert stumbling upon someone to guide them at last. He desperately fought the urge to cling to her. "Kurumi, listen to me. Something's weird in this world. Origami's—"

"A Spirit. Yes, I know," she said, speaking over him.

He stared at her, stunned. "…! You knew?"

"Yes." She nodded. "Although I only found out a little earlier myself."

"You did…?" He hung his head slightly before continuing. "Why…? Why on earth did it turn out like this? Does it mean something happened to Origami?"

"That is also a bit of a trial for me to understand. Buuuut…," she said, doing a little spin where she stood. "With Origami as she is now, there are ways we can find this out."

"R-really?"

"Yes." She smiled and brought her heel down onto the roof as if taking a step. The shadow that pooled at her feet slithered up to cover her body and produce a red-and-black garment. Her Astral Dress. A Spirit's armor and castle.

He turned wary eyes on her abruptly manifesting this powerful shield.

"Hee-hee-hee! Please don't be so frightened," she told him as she held up her right hand. A pistol leaped out of the shadows and tucked itself into that hand. Licking her lips, she continued. "If I shoot Origami with this tenth bullet, Yud, I can learn what kind of life she's led in this world. Well, needless to say, it won't tell me *every* little thing, but if we narrow down the focus to what led her to become a Spirit, I believe we can obtain the desired information."

"Yud…? We can?!" Shido stared in disbelief. Yud. That was the bullet that conveyed to Kurumi the target's memories of the past. With it, they could find out what had happened to Origami.

"But then couldn't you have used Yud to find out why Origami inverted in the original world?" he asked, without meaning much of anything.

"Well, in theory, yes, that would be the case." She shrugged theatrically. "That is, *if* I could have approached that Origami and fired the bullet."

"Unh…" He felt his face tense. It was true that the original inverted Origami hadn't really given them the luxury of such leisurely action. "A-anyway, now we can find out why Origami inverted in this world, right? Please, Kurumi. You gotta help me!"

"Hee-hee-hee! Well, let me see." Kurumi touched the barrel of the gun to her lips, bemused.

Origami had started out on her way home after classes ended, but then returned to Raizen High School for one reason. She noticed that the pin she always wore in her hair had disappeared at some point. It was only a small pin, and normally such a thing wouldn't have been worth the effort of trying to find. But seeing as how this pin had been given to her by her mother a long time ago, it was a different story.

That said, however, she didn't know exactly where it had fallen out. In the end, she'd traced her steps back to the high school, climbed the stairs, gone down the hallway, looked around the classroom, and gone to the stairs up to the roof where she'd talked with Shido Itsuka at lunch.

"Oh! There it is!" She crouched and scooped the pin off the floor. It must have fallen out while she was talking with Shido. Probably when she'd taken his hand excitedly after she found out he was the little brother of that boy who saved her parents.

"I have to be more careful," she murmured to herself as she wiped the pin off with her fingers and put it in her hair. From the corner of her eye, she saw something move suddenly. "Hmm?"

She looked over and spotted two people on the roof through the window in the door. One was her classmate, Shido Itsuka. And the other was wearing a red-and-black Astral Dress, the Spirit Nightmare.

"Ah..." The moment she registered their presence, her mind went black, like the power had abruptly cut out.

"Huh?" Shido heard the squeak of the door to the roof opening. He looked that way to find a girl standing there with her head hanging. "Is that...Origami?"

Yes. Because her head was hanging, he hadn't been sure for a second, but this girl was without a doubt Origami Tobiichi. Class was over, so what was she doing up here?

He was about to pose that very question when he stopped short with a gasp. The reason was simple—he had remembered the Spirit on the roof with him, Kurumi.

In this world as well, Origami had belonged to the AST. Which meant a non-zero possibility that she had come face-to-face with Kurumi before. At the very least, she would have seen the videos.

"O-Origami, so, like, this is, uh," he said, trying to smooth this over.

He'd only just gotten her to meet with him, and he didn't need her getting any weird ideas now.

But she appeared to not even have heard him speak; head hanging, arms dangling by her sides, she slowly moved forward.

"Origami?" He called her name dubiously.

"Oh my, oh dear?" Kurumi furrowed her brow. And then for a moment she was dyed black, as though swallowed by a shadow, before the color quickly returned to her. "I suppose this is the first time we've officially met in this world, Origami? Although perhaps we've run into each other before—?"

"Spi. Rit," Origami said quietly, interrupting Kurumi, and an inky darkness spun out around her like a spider's web. It looked as though night had abruptly fallen around her alone.

Shido's eyes automatically widened at this anomaly. "Wha—?!"

This vortex of darkness whirled around Origami to weave a dress of mourning. It was without a doubt…

"Astral Dress?!" he cried, stunned.

Yes. The Origami who had appeared on the roof was clad in a Spirit's armor, Astral Dress. And it was not the bridal outfit he'd witnessed previously, but rather the inky-black post-inversion garb.

Instantly, a wave of tension and pressure swept through the area and made it hard to breathe. His legs trembled ever so slightly, and he would've collapsed on the spot if he hadn't been bracing himself.

But this was, of course, perfectly natural. The Demon King, the tremendously powerful avatar of destruction. *This* was what was manifesting before his eyes at that very moment.

"So you *are* Devil, then?!" he cried, but she didn't respond.

However, now that he had seen her like this, this was the only possible conclusion. At the very least, he had apparently not been mistaken about her being Devil. So did that mean she had been lying to him?

He hadn't thought so at the time, but… He shivered in fear as his thoughts raced.

"Shido," Kurumi said abruptly. "It might be dangerous to remain in that position."

In the next second, a number of dark masses appeared around the silent Origami, expanded, and coalesced into what appeared to be massive feathers.

He'd seen these before. They were the inverted form of the Angel that had rained beams of light on the city, wreaking havoc and ruin in the original world.

"...Satan...," Origami murmured, and the innumerable feathers turned their tips toward Shido and Kurumi.

"...!" He froze in place; everything was happening too fast. And then he found himself falling to one side. A heartbeat later, he realized that Kurumi had pushed him. "Ngh!"

By the time he registered this, Kurumi had already leaped into the sky. The light beams grazed the school building in the spot where she'd been standing until only a fraction of a second earlier, shot through the fence, and plunged off into the distance.

"That is *quite* the violent hello!" Kurumi shouted and pulled the trigger on the pistol in her hand. A bullet like solidified shadow came from the barrel and charged at Origami.

But some of the feathers floating around the other Spirit came together like a shield and easily defended against the blow, while the remaining feathers turned their tips toward Kurumi in the sky.

"Hngh—" Inky beams shot toward the defenseless Kurumi and pierced her chest and abdomen, severed her head and limbs from her body. The slender girl was instantly rendered down to sad remains.

"Kurumi?!" Shido shouted.

Almost in response, what had been Kurumi until a moment ago tumbled in pieces from the sky, crumbling like coal as they hit the roof.

"O-Origami, you—" He wrenched his gaze away from this tragic sight and looked toward the other girl. "Huh?"

He was stunned. Because after killing Kurumi, Origami knelt lifelessly on the spot, and the feathers floating around her broke up into tiny particles and faded away. And then the black Astral Dress wrapped around her body melted into the air, and she was back in her usual school uniform.

As if her objective had been achieved when Kurumi died.

"What…the…?" Shido stared, stupefied, unable to process what had just happened.

Before too long, Origami slowly raised her face. "Hmm? Itsuka?" she said with a blank look when she spotted him. "What are you doing up here?"

"Huh?" This unexpected response only increased his confusion.

Her face and tone were so completely innocent and free of malice, it was almost impossible to believe that she had just shot Kurumi down. If this was an act, then she could have easily gone on to become the most celebrated actor in history, or a swindling mastermind.

"What even *is* this?" Shido murmured, dazed, and Origami cocked her head to one side, confused. But rather than responding to his words, she seemed to be trying to remember why she herself was on the roof.

"It…happened again?" she said in a quiet voice, and she stood up, brushing the dirt off her knees.

"Again?" he parroted. "Wh-what happened again?"

"Huh? Oh… You heard that?" Origami scratched her head awkwardly. "The truth is, for a little while now, I've been blacking out sometimes. I think it's probably low blood sugar or something."

"Blacking out?" He frowned and swallowed hard.

She looked him curiously before letting out a little "Oh!" as if she had just remembered something. "Um. Anyway. Did you read the note I passed you in class?"

"Huh? O-oh," he replied. "Yeah, I read it."

Origami whirled around. "Um, so that's…that's how it is," she said, leaving the roof on quick feet.

"Ah—" He was too slow in calling out to stop her. She slipped inside the building and marched down the stairs.

Left alone on the roof, all he could do was stand rooted to the spot in a daze.

Origami had shown up, turned into an inverted Spirit, killed Kurumi, and walked off, like nothing had happened. The whole thing probably hadn't even taken five full minutes. But in that brief interval, the world around Shido had changed significantly.

"Kurumi…" He murmured her name.

"Yes, yes, you called?" A shadow loomed beside Shido, and the very girl who had been killed by Origami popped her face out from inside it.

"…" He simply stared at her.

"Oh my!" she cooed. "You are not terribly surprised?"

"Something like this happened once before," he told her, running his hands through his hair. She had probably switched with an avatar when Origami first showed up. "I hate the way you use up avatars like that. I mean, I know they're avatars, but they're still alive, right?"

"Hee-hee-hee! You are so awfully kind, Shido," she replied. "But there is no need for concern. If I use Het, I could re-create even that me which was killed just now."

"…"

Without a word, he let out a long sigh. The way he and Kurumi thought about life was just too different.

She apparently had no intention of discussing the matter further. Changing the subject, she turned her eyes to the door through which Origami had disappeared. "What did you think about Origami there?"

"What did I think? I mean…" He shrugged. To be honest, there were too many unknowns to grapple with. A troubled look on his face, he put a hand to his chin. "Well, one thing's certain. It'll be tough to get information using Yud. I guess."

"I suppose so, hmm?" Kurumi agreed.

He didn't know what state this Origami was in, but she had definitely changed into a Spirit at the sight of Kurumi. Given that fact, it would be a trial getting anywhere near her.

"Why did it turn out like this?" he asked, pained. "Was I—was what I did a mistake?"

Kurumi sighed. "I don't think so. If you hadn't saved her parents, the Tengu of this world would have also been mercilessly razed by the inverted Origami. Considering that, the current situation is not the worst outcome. Don't you agree?"

"I—I guess maybe," he stammered. It wasn't like he didn't get what Kurumi was saying. Considering what had happened in his original world, this current one could have been said to be still mostly peaceful.

But he couldn't quite get on board with that. What had happened to Origami? He couldn't stop wondering about it.

Perhaps seeing this question in his face, Kurumi giggled. "Well, I did expect your thoughts to go in that direction, Shido. Although I'm also interested in how the world would be overwritten when one incident is changed."

"...! Then—," Shido started to say, and then he stopped. Because Kurumi held up a finger and pressed it to his lips.

"Buuuut," she said, the corners of her mouth stretching up into a grin. "I am not so good-natured as that, you see. Anything further will require an extra *fee*, hmm?"

Shido unconsciously gasped at the lurid smile on her face.

"Hee-hee!" She shrugged and did another little spin. "Well then, I'll be on my way. We will, of course, meet again, Shido." She disappeared into the shadows, leaving only those words in her wake.

"So..." Kotori said, flicking up the stick of the Chupa Chups in her mouth and fixing him with a glare. She had ambushed him in black-ribboned commander mode when he got home. "You have some explaining to do, right, Shido?"

Shido understood the reason for the interrogation only too well— Origami.

There were three people currently in the living room of the Itsuka house. One was Shido, the second was Kotori, and the third was a woman with a sleepy face, who already had a small terminal ready to go in her hand. This was Ratatoskr analyst, Reine Murasame.

"Y-you're here, too, Reine?" he asked.

"...Mm." She nodded. "Think of me as a secretary. Although I can go if this doesn't work for you."

"No, it's nothing like that," he said, scratching his cheek. Given that Tohka, Yoshino, and the other Spirits were nowhere to be seen, they had most likely been given clear instructions to be on standby in the apartment building.

"Now, Shido." Kotori jerked her chin up, as if to urge him on.

"R-right," he stammered, overwhelmed by the heavy air hanging over the room. He had indeed said that he would explain the situation after he got home, so he could get Ratatoskr's help. But now that the time had finally come, he struggled with how to explain everything that had happened.

"Hmph." Kotori sniffed her displeasure. "So *now* you can't talk, is that it? Or are you worried I won't get what you have to say? You do me wrong. Do I seem *that* unreliable a commander to you, Shido?"

"No, I didn't mean to..." He shook his head, and Kotori pursed her lips sulkily.

"You could have at least a little faith in me...Big Bro," she said in a quiet voice.

"...!" Shido opened his eyes wide with a gasp. And then, shoving his hands into his hair, he let out a sigh.

"You're right. Sorry, Kotori," he said, like an admonishment to himself, and bowed his head slightly. What exactly was he so worried about? The girl before him was much smarter than he was and much stronger. "You might think it's totally absurd, but everything I'm about to tell you is the truth. Will you hear me out?"

Instantly, Kotori's face brightened. But then her eyebrows dropped, and she returned to commander mode as she nodded. "Yes, of course."

Shido smiled wryly at this change in her and began to tell his story. About how he'd known this girl, Origami; how she'd turned into a Spirit and then inverted and destroyed the city; how in order to prevent that, he had gone back five years using Kurumi's power to rewind time and changed the path the world would have gone down by saving Origami's parents; and how Origami existed in this world as the Spirit, Devil, anyway.

He calmly recounted to Kotori and Reine what he'd experienced. The whole telling probably took fifteen minutes.

"And that's about it," he finished.

"..."

Kotori sniffed and then dipped her head slightly. "Overwrite the world. I see. I finally understand why you've been so weird since yesterday." She put a hand to her chin. "Well, at any rate, I'll go ahead and believe you. I can't think of any reason you'd tell me a lie like that. And..." She signaled Reine with her eyes.

"...Mm," Reine said, and tapped at the screen she held before turning it toward Shido and Kotori.

"Hmm?" He peered at it and then gasped.

It showed the inverted Origami standing on the roof of the high school. He could also see himself and Kurumi on one edge of the screen. The exact situation he'd been in earlier that day.

"This is..." He stared in amazement.

"Yes. Video captured by an autonomous camera this evening. I had a number of cameras flying around looking for information on Origami Tobiichi, but I never dreamed I'd get to see a decisive moment like this." Kotori looked at him in consternation. "There's no mistake that Origami Tobiichi is Devil. But she herself isn't aware of that. I had Reine analyze her parameters, and it doesn't look like she was lying to you."

"Meaning she...?" he started to ask, and Kotori answered before he could finish the question.

"Yes. It's possible that Origami Tobiichi hasn't realized she's become a Spirit."

He gasped. "Is that even possible?"

She shrugged. "It's a pattern we haven't seen before. But given that we have a real-life example right here before our eyes, we can't deny that it's true. I have no idea how this would happen, though."

Reine sighed as she stroked her chin and tapped at her terminal. "... Do you mind if I?"

"Mm." Kotori gave her a slight nod. "What is it, Reine?"

"...Mm. This is at most a hypothesis, a theory, but there is one point in Shin's story I have a question about."

"A question?" Shido asked. "What is it?"

"…You succeeded in changing things, Shin," Reine continued. "And no one remembers the original world…yes?"

"Yeah." He nodded. "Kurumi and I are the only ones who know about the original world."

"…That's the thing."

"Huh?" He cocked his head to one side, and Reine raised a finger.

"…I wonder why you and Kurumi alone would have memories of the original world. With Kurumi, it might be due to her powers, but I don't understand why you would remember, Shin."

"Hmm." Now that she mentioned it, that was true. He'd sort of just gone with it because he was the person who had done the changing of the world, but now that he was here, he should have been the Shido living in this newly constructed world. He didn't have a clear reason why he would have no memories of this and still have them of the original world.

"…Most likely, some kind of conditions have to be met in order to have memories from the original world," Reine suggested.

"Conditions?" He frowned. "Like what exactly?"

"…I don't know for sure. If we say that Kurumi is an exception, then the sample size is just too small. But for instance, what if the condition was being shot with Yud Bet by Kurumi or having Spirit power?"

"Uh." Shido had a perplexed look on his face, while Kotori across from him opened her eyes wide in understanding.

"Oh! Right!" she said. "If there are multiple conditions, then it's possible Origami Tobiichi remembered the original world the moment Phantom gave her Spirit power. Regardless of the fact she only had memories of *this* world until that point!"

"Oh!" It finally clicked into place for Shido. "W-wait just a minute, Reine. So then you're saying inverted Origami is the Origami who got back her memory of the original world?!"

Reine quietly lowered her eyes. "…I told you, it's a theory at best. Nothing more than a possibility. But it is a fact it all starts to make sense when you think about it this way."

"B-but," he protested. "When she came to school, Origami was regular—I mean, she was the Origami with memories of this world, you know?"

"...We can't know the details without asking Kurumi, but unlike you and the way you had memories of the original world from the start, Origami had memories of this world," Reine continued. "So what if this information, the memories of the original world, were forced into her, what would happen? At the very least, I doubt it would have a positive impact on the host of those memories. Is it not possible to think that in order to protect herself, the Origami with memories of this world and the Origami with memories of the original world split? And we could also assume that the switch to call up the Origami with memories of the original world is..."

"The presence of a Spirit, hmm?" Kotori said, flicking the stick of her Chupa Chups up.

Reine nodded. "...Most likely, yes. When we look at the fact that she didn't react to Tohka in the classroom, she might be displaying a reaction to Spirit *power* rather than to Spirits themselves. In which case, it would be extremely dangerous to manifest a limited Astral Dress in front of her."

Indeed, Origami had only turned into a Spirit when she saw Kurumi. And after killing Kurumi, she had immediately returned to being the usual Origami.

"B-but assuming that's true, then what on earth are we—?" he started to say in a shaky voice, and Kotori cut him off sharply.

"What are you talking about? Sure, we're up against the most malevolent and vicious inverted Spirit, Devil. But if you look at it another way, although she's got immense Spirit power, she won't turn into a Spirit unless specific conditions are met."

"I—I just...," Shido said, clenching his hands into fists. Kotori was exactly right. They'd get nowhere running away.

"It is an irregular case, but now that we know Origami Tobiichi is Devil, there's just one thing for Ratatoskr to do." Kotori turned her gaze on Shido.

He didn't need her to spell it out. His lips stretched into a smile, and he nodded.

Ratatoskr's doctrine was to nullify the Spirits that were the cause of the spacequakes, using peaceful means. And to that end, they had to use a particular method—date them and make them weak in the knees.

Kotori nodded with satisfaction at his reaction and then grabbed the stick of the Chupa Chups in her mouth between two fingers and snapped it out at Shido. "And! So! Now that that's settled, we move first thing tomorrow. Shido, you contact Origami somehow and ask her out on a date. Sometime this week at the very latest."

"Right. I'm on it." And then he remembered. "Oh!"

"What is it?" Kotori arched an eyebrow at him.

"I already did ask her out," he told her slowly. "She said she's free on Saturday."

"Hah?!" She yelped loudly. His response had apparently been entirely unexpected. "H-how? You mean you hit on her before the measurements came back? *You?*"

"U-uh. I wasn't actually hitting on her…"

"So then how'd the date thing come up?"

"Well, that was…" He was at a loss for how to reply to that.

"Mm-hmmmm." She stared at him with hard eyes and stroked his chin, like a kitten playing with a mouse. "Looks like I'll need to hear a liiiittle bit about what kind of relationship you and Origami Tobiichi had in the original world."

"Wh-what…?" The color drained from his face.

"Aaaah." Origami squirmed and rolled around on her bed that night, clutching a long body pillow.

The reason was simple. Thinking back on how she'd acted throughout the day was embarrassing. Sure, that boy had asked her out, but answering like that was just too much. And seeing him again on the roof after that was the icing on the cake. The whole thing made her want to snap at herself, *What shoujo manga do you think you're starring in?*

She sighed, rolled onto her back, and stared absently at the ceiling.

That boy, Shido Itsuka. She really was surprised when she saw his face. He really was the spitting image of the boy etched deeply into her memory, the one who had sacrificed himself to save her parents five years earlier. Maybe that was why the moment she saw his face, she'd been overcome with deep emotion.

No. It wasn't only that.

When she heard his voice, when she smelled his scent, when she touched his hands, she'd felt an indescribable emotion in her heart. What on earth was it? It definitely wasn't unpleasant. But it was a strange feeling, like being tickled on the inside.

"It can't actually be *that*, could it?" she said quietly. An unknown emotion. Feelings she'd never felt before. What if this was…?

Her phone buzzed next to her pillow, announcing the arrival of a message.

"…!" She jolted up, as if propelled by the electronic sound.

She took a couple deep breaths, as if to calm herself, before reaching a hand toward her phone. She looked at the screen and saw that the sender was Shido himself.

"…!" Her heart started pounding, and she didn't get why. But she couldn't stay frozen in place like this. She took another deep breath, tapped at the screen, and let her eyes crawl over the message. It was an apology for the sudden invite that day, a bit about how he was very delighted to be able to get to see her again, and a time and meeting spot for Saturday.

"Wha?! Whoa!" She tossed the phone back and forth in her hands like she was holding a hot potato and began to roll around on her bed with frantic energy. She was way too worked up. The inside of her head was total chaos, even though all that had happened was that she'd gotten a text from a boy she'd met that day.

"…! Right. Answer him." She finally hit upon this course of action only after dancing frenetically for a minute or two. She tapped at her phone. "The meeting spot and time sound good. There…"

Was this answer really all right? Wasn't it actually way too brief? What if he saw this overly businesslike reply and lost all interest in her and decided to give up on the whole thing on Saturday…?

" "
…

Silently, Origami deleted the sentence, straightened up, and wrote a new message. She neatly replied to each sentence in Shido's message, spelling out with ample lyrical expression how glad she was he'd reached out to her, how she couldn't wait for Saturday, and how she got a strange feeling when she thought about him.

"Way too girly!" Halfway through, she grew embarrassed and deleted the text again, her cheeks coloring red.

By the time she finally managed to compose an acceptable response, it was the next day.

Saturday, November 11. Shido was walking along the road to Tengu Station alone.

The sky was clear. Although the air itself was chilly, the sun was warm, and it didn't seem like the sun of approaching winter. It was the perfect weather for a date.

"Aren't you a little early, though? You're meeting at eleven, right?" He heard Kotori's voice through the small transmitter in his right ear. This earpiece was connected with the airship *Fraxinus*, hanging approximately 15,000 meters above the spot where he was now. The crew assembled on its bridge would be providing backup for his date that day.

"No," he replied in a quiet voice as he glanced at his phone. 10:12. He had forty-eight minutes until they were supposed to meet. "I wouldn't be surprised if Origami's there already. Of course, I can't say for sure because this Origami is slightly different from the one I know, but… isn't this better than making her wait a long time?"

"You sure do know a lot about her. For just *a classmate,"* Kotori said, her voice thorny.

A pained smile crossed his face as sweat trickled down his cheek. That's what he'd said when she'd demanded to know his relationship with Origami in the original world, but it was clear that she didn't fully believe it.

"If we're going back to the start of things, you guys are the reason

I got to know Origami at all," he grumbled into his earpiece. In fact, although there had been the events of five years earlier, he had actually started talking to Origami with some frequency because he'd been trying to pick her up in the "training" Kotori had insisted on. He'd told her all about that, but…

"No idea what you're going on about there."

"Hngh." He gritted his teeth, at a loss for how to respond. The Kotori of this world had no memory of anything like that.

While they were talking, he arrived at the plaza in front of the station. He was meeting Origami by the fountain there. It was the same meeting spot as when he'd been forced to triple-book a date with her, Tohka, and Kurumi.

"Ah." Entering the plaza, he let out a short cry and stopped in his tracks. Origami was already standing in front of the fountain. That said, however, he wasn't particularly surprised to find her there. The reason he'd stopped was her outfit.

Cardigan over a blouse with a cute design, skirt in a fall color. It was a girly style that the Origami in his memory hadn't worn, and it automatically caught his eye.

"Shido?" Kotori called out to him, and he gasped.

"…! R-right."

"Haah." He heard her sigh. *"I've got my concerns about this."*

"S-sorry."

"Please focus. I don't know what it was like in the original world, but at the very least, the person you're looking at right this very instant is the Spirit hunter, Devil," she warned. *"Who knows what'll happen if you let your guard down? You have to take on this challenge like you were facing Kurumi Tokisaki."*

He took a few deep breaths to get his pounding heart under control and then nodded his head. "Yeah. I got it."

"Good. Now, then. Shall we begin our date?" she said, announcing the start of the mission.

At the same time, Shido started to move again and headed for the fountain.

Origami jerked her head up with a surprised look on her face. "Itsuka? You're early."

"Ha-ha!" he laughed. "I guess I could say the same about you?"

She looked at the clock in the plaza and then shrugged awkwardly. "Um. I didn't want to keep you waiting."

"Aah, I actually thought the same thing," he replied, and her eyes grew wider. Then they both started laughing.

"Thank you so much for the kind invitation today, Itsuka," she said, sounding stilted. "Um, this is a little embarrassing, but I've never gone out alone with a boy before, so I might be a bit awkward."

"N-no, no." He shook his head. "I mean, it's not like I have any experience, either."

"Can't believe you can say that with a straight face, after taking down so many Spirits," Kotori snarked through the earpiece.

"Sh-shut it," he snapped.

Origami cocked her head curiously to one side. "Did you say something, Itsuka?"

"No, nothing." He hurriedly waved it away. "Anyway, we're classmates and all. You can skip the formalities, you know?"

"But," she protested.

"Come on, it kind of puts me on edge. Please," he said, pressing his hands together with a pleading look.

Her eyebrows rose into an inverted V for a moment before she finally nodded firmly in agreement. "I understa—I mean, got it."

"Ha-ha!" His cheeks automatically softened at this more familiar tone. "That's more like it, Origami."

"Huh?" She let out a baffled cry, and he realized that he had unconsciously called her by her first name again.

"Oh, sorry. I didn't mean to call you that. Um. It's just, it's a beautiful name," he said, trying to deflect. It wasn't a lie, but the truth was, he was just used to calling her by name in the original world. He had normally called her Tobiichi, but at some point, he'd gotten used to using her first name.

She seemed unsettled somehow, but she didn't appear to have taken offense. Her face softened, and a smile crossed her lips. "Thanks. I'm glad my mom and dad gave it to me."

"That makes sense." He felt a complex mix of emotions at the words "mom and dad."

But Origami apparently didn't notice this, and she averted her eyes slightly. "So if you want to call me that, Itsuka, it's…all right."

"Huh?" He gaped at her.

"Origami, I mean," she said, her cheeks coloring faintly, and all he could do was stare.

"*Shido, why aren't you saying anything?!*" Kotori yelled. "*She's taking a serious step toward you!*"

"Ah…" He hurried to string words together. "Th-thanks…Origami," he said, averting his eyes a bit in the same way as Origami had. The name came out so naturally before, but now that he had formally been given permission, he felt a little awkward using it.

"Mm-hmm." She smiled.

"Oh. So then, right. You can call me Shido," he suggested. "It'd be unfair otherwise."

"What?" The look on her face was one of surprise. And then she stammered, "Shi…d—" She stopped in the middle and scratched her cheek uncomfortably. "Maybe once I get used to it. Okay?"

"What? Oh. O-of course!" he agreed, and there was silence for a few seconds.

"*Shido, it's not really great to be quiet for too long. Anything's fine, just please keep the conversation going,*" Kotori instructed. And she was right.

He searched for a topic in his head. "So, like," he said, at the same time as Origami opened her mouth.

"So."

A curious embarrassment came over both of them.

Origami was the first to push past it. Returning her gaze to Shido, she asked, "Anyway, what are we doing today, Itsuka?"

"Huh?"

"Sorry. But you only told me the time and place to meet."

"A-ah, right. Today—," he started to say, when he heard a familiar ringing in his ear for the first time in a while.

Ratatoskr's cream of the crop were seated alongside each other on the bridge of the airship *Fraxinus* 15,000 meters in the air above the city of Tengu. These were the romance masters selected from across the nation to provide backup for Shido under Kotori's command. Maintaining an ideal level of tension, they turned their eyes to the enormous main monitor set up on the bridge.

Shown there was a video feed from the ground sent by autonomous cameras. It showed the target Origami Tobiichi from the waist up from Shido's viewpoint, and displayed around this main image were videos at angles captured by different cameras, together with a variety of parameter displays.

And now the second Origami asked her question, there was a loud beeping on the bridge, and a window opened up on-screen.

"Here we go! Options!" Kotori slapped her knee where she sat in the captain's chair on the upper level of the bridge as she flicked the stick of her Chupa Chups up and down and up and down.

Fraxinus's onboard AI measured the changes in the target's emotional indices and displayed three options for action for Shido to take at that time.

1. "ACTUALLY, THERE'S THIS MOVIE I WANT TO SEE WITH YOU." ROMANTIC FILM AT THE THEATER.

2. "I THOUGHT WE COULD GO SHOPPING." FUN SHOPPING TRIP.

3. "HOW ABOUT WE QUIT BEATING AROUND THE BUSH?" STRAIGHT TO A LOVE HOTEL.

"Choices, people!" Kotori ordered, and the crew pushed the buttons before them as one.

The aggregate results were displayed on the main monitor, with the most votes being for two.

"Hmm. Two, huh? I guess that *is* the safe option," Kotori said, stroking her chin.

"I'm reluctant to discard one," a crew member said from the lower deck. That was Bad Marriage Kawagoe. "But I'm also concerned about putting them into a place with no conversation right from the get-go."

Next, as if to show her agreement, Deep Love Minowa opened her mouth. "In that respect, two is the option with the most versatility. It's a reasonable option in the sense that it will allow us to see how things develop. There isn't a girl alive who hates shopping."

Everyone agreed that they had no objections to this.

Nail Knocker Shiizaki looked pale. "Why...would an option like three come up right out of the gate...?"

"We can't know that without asking the *Fraxinus* AI," Kotori said with a shrug. In fact, during the Tohka mission, the AI had led Shido and Tohka to a "rest" hotel, but this was at best because she had been a Spirit who was unfamiliar with this world. (Incidentally, were Shido to have proceeded beyond a kiss, they had Ratatoskr personnel placed there disguised as cleaning staff.)

But this target was a formerly human Spirit. Meaning there was a strong possibility that she knew exactly what kind of facility the love hotel was. If he tried to take her to a place like that on their first date, he wouldn't have much of a leg to stand on after she slapped him in the face.

Kotori pulled the mic to her. "Shido, it's settled. Two—"

"*Hang on a second,*" he interrupted her in a whisper too quiet for Origami to hear.

"What is it?"

"*There's something I want to try with this set of options.*"

"Huh?" Her eyes grew wide at how unusually serious he sounded. This was the first time he'd ever made a request like this. But she quickly realized how unique this Spirit was, this girl, Origami Tobiichi.

According to Shido, the world had gone down a different path due to events five years earlier. In a different possible world, Shido and Origami had been friendly. In which case, it made sense that he might have known about inclinations of Origami's that Kotori and her crew had not grasped.

After thinking it over for a moment, she flicked the stick of her Chupa Chups up. "Okay. Just this once. Go ahead and choose the option you like, Shido."

"..." He tapped his earpiece to indicate his understanding.

She turned her gaze back to Origami on the main monitor.

"Hey, Origami?" Shido said. "*There's actually somewhere I want to go. Is that cool?*"

"*Sure, that's fine,*" she agreed and began walking alongside him.

They'd gone a little ways when he stopped abruptly.

"*Huh?*" Origami gaped as she looked up at the building before them.

But that was entirely understandable. Shido had led her to what appeared to be a castle with a prominent sign noting the amounts for an overnight stay and for a shorter "rest."

A shrill alarm began to blare on the bridge of the airship. At the same time, Mr. President Mikimoto and Dimension Breaker Nakatsugawa, who had been looking at their personal monitors, cried out in a panic.

"Emotional indices are unstable!"

"Origami Tobiichi is upset!"

"Well, of *course* she is! The hell are you thinking, Shidooooooo?!" Kotori roared, yanking the mic toward her. "Shido! Make some kind of excuse before Origami gets mad!"

"*Huh? No, but—*"

"Just do it. Before it's too late!" she barked.

Shido looked uncertain for an instant before turning to Origami with a smile. "*Okay, it's here. Just over here.*"

"*Oh.*" Origami let out a sigh of relief. "*It's not* this *place.*"

"*W-well, yeah. Come on, let's go.*"

"O-okay."

He led her past the hotel, and the alarm finally stopped ringing.

"Haah." Kotori let out a sigh of relief and wiped the sweat from her brow. "Honestly. What were you *thinking*, Shido? You take a girl to a place like that on your first date, and you're practically *asking* her to run away screaming."

"Sorry," he replied in a quiet voice, looking very much like this wasn't quite making sense to him. *"I figured Origami would definitely want to come here, so..."*

"No, wait. Meaning what?" she replied, her face stiffening. She had no idea what would make him connect Origami with a love hotel. "At any rate, go with two. We're going shopping."

"Roger." Shido nodded and began to suggest to Origami that they go shopping.

Watching this on the main monitor, Kotori spoke to her crew on the lower deck. "So how's likability with Origami? I hope it hasn't gone down too much."

"C-Commander." Nakatsugawa adjusted his glasses with a baffled look. "There was significant fluctuation in the emotional indices, but...likability hasn't decreased in the slightest. In fact, it seems to have *increased* a tiny bit?"

"...What?" Kotori asked dubiously.

Shido slipped through an alley with Origami and came out onto the main road.

As they walked, Origami abruptly asked, "So then where are we going?"

"Oh, I thought we could go shopping," he replied, and she cocked her head to one side.

"To buy what?"

"Oh... Um..." Now that she mentioned it, what they would shop for hadn't been decided. He scratched his cheek as he thought it over.

"Wait. We've got some choices here." He heard Kotori through the earpiece, and an automated voice read out the list of options.

*   *   *

There were three choices displayed on the bridge's main monitor.

1. Let her pick out an outfit at a boutique.

2. Play with the animals at a pet shop and grow closer.

3. Go to a shady pharmacy with powerful energy drinks and aphrodisiacs.

"All hands! Choices!" Kotori shouted, and the aggregate totals were displayed on the monitor.

One got the most votes, with two coming in a close second. Naturally, there were no votes for three.

"One, hmm? I agree." She nodded, satisfied.

"Well, it's a reasonable compromise," one crew member noted.

"Two isn't bad, either," came the voice of another. "But not everyone loves animals."

"Why would three even be in there? I feel like that's quite specific," Kawagoe said with a frown. Indeed, the nature of that option alone was quite separate.

Kotori didn't really understand what the AI was thinking. Maybe she needed to perform a system overhaul? "Shido, did you hear that?" she said. "The reasonable one here is one—"

"It's gotta be three." Shido's voice came through the speaker sounding like this was the utterly obvious choice.

"Uh?" She automatically furrowed her brow. "What are you talking about, Shido? Be reasonable. That is very clearly not a place a girl her age would go!"

"No, but, I mean, we're talking about Origami," he protested.

"Meaning what exactly?!" she shrieked. She didn't get it.

"Meaning, it's hard to say, but... It's kind of like, Origami and energy

drinks go together like milk and cookies, you know?" he said, sounding like he was making a common-sense statement.

Kotori placed a hand on her head. "No, hang on here. I seriously don't get it. What kind of girl was this Origami Tobiichi you knew, anyway?"

"Huh? The kind of girl who'd make you drink a weird cocktail of energy drinks, set a trap to keep you from escaping her house, lick your neck when you were carrying her on your back—"

"What?! Are you pulling my leg? There's no way a girl like that actually exists!"

"I—I mean, she did, though." Shido frowned in consternation. Apparently, this really was not a joke. He was being serious.

Kotori recalled the movement in Origami Tobiichi's likability earlier. Although she had been upset at the truly unexpected choice, her likability had not dropped. What if maybe…?

She pulled her thoughts together in two seconds and snorted slightly. "Fine. Give it a try."

"Commander?!"

Shocked cries came from the deck below. But she continued speaking, her eyes on the main monitor.

"However! If her likability drops even a smidge or her emotional levels turn unstable, you switch to one immediately. Got it?"

"Y-yeah, got it," he replied, leading Origami into a back alley.

"Woh-kay. Pretty sure this is it." Shido stopped in front of a pharmacy.

"Huh?" Origami opened her eyes wide in surprise.

But that only made sense. Even at a glance, the place looked like nothing other than an ordinary mixed-use building. But when they went inside and up to the second floor, there was a pharmacy decked out like a haunted house. It was the sort of secret spot you'd never find if you were just going about your daily business. Shido himself would have never even been able to lead her there if she hadn't informed him of the existence of the place in the original world.

The shop was crammed full of bottles and packages like nothing she'd ever seen in a regular drugstore, and the writing on the labels was very clearly not in Japanese. This was easily one of the shadiest stores.

"What kind of store *is* this?" she asked, a dubious look on her face.

Of course, Shido couldn't retort that she was a regular here, so he fumbled for an appropriate reply. "Well, let's just take a look around. If you don't really like it, we'll go somewhere else."

"O-okay..." She stared at the questionable bottles of medicine that lined the shelves. But it seemed like it wasn't really connecting for her, and she cocked her head to one side.

Maybe her interests really were different from those of the Origami he knew. In which case, maybe he should change plans sooner rather than later, like Kotori had said. She told him to go look at clothes for Origami, right? And if the target was an average girl, then that sort of thing would definitely have been the right choice.

"Itsuka?" she called out to him. "I actually... I don't really get it, I think. Can we go somewhere else?"

"O-oh, yeah? Sorry, I just—" Shido stopped, abruptly.

The reason was simple. The products lining the shelves had raised Origami's eyebrows like a tent above her eyes. But at some point, she'd picked up a basket and filled it with the strongest-looking energy drinks and aphrodisiacs in the shop.

"Origami, are you...?" He pointed at the basket.

"Huh?" Her eyes flew open like she hadn't even noticed the basket before that moment. "I—I... When on earth did I...?" She pressed a hand to her forehead and staggered as if dizzy.

"A-are you okay?" He hurried over to hold her up and heard a piercing alarm through his earpiece.

"*Shido!*" Kotori cried. "*Origami's emotion index is making an insane waveform!*"

"A-anyway, how about we get out of here?! Sound good?!" Shido led the tottering Origami out of the shop.

Soon after, she finally regained her composure. "Sorry, Itsuka. I have no idea what happened to me back there. Weird."

"W-well, don't worry about it. It's my bad for bringing you to such a weird store," he told her. "I know! If you want, how about we go look at clothes next?"

She nodded, and then the two of them set out down the road once more.

But here Shido scratched his cheek. He had no issue with going to look at clothes, but he didn't know what kind of store Origami would like. He was pretty sure that in the original world, she had mentioned something about buying pretty much all of her clothes online.

"So then where do you usually go to shop, Origami?" he asked.

"Hmm. I guess I mostly get my clothes in my neighborhood." She smiled, slightly embarrassed. "I know I should actually be more into clothes, but I'm not great with fashion. I don't really have any style."

"That's not true," he protested. "Your outfit today's pretty cute."

"...!" She got a surprised look on her face and averted her eyes.

"Origami?"

"Mm-hmm." She shook her head. "It's nothing. A-anyway, if we're going to look at clothes, then could we go to the station building? I know that means retracing our steps a bit, but I almost never go there."

"Oh, sure," he agreed. They slipped out of the alley and began walking down the main road toward the station.

"*Hmm. I wondered for a sec how that was going to play out, but it seems like it's not too bad.*" He heard Kotori's voice in his right ear. "*Likability's looking great, too. We play our cards right, and we might even be able to settle this today. But don't let your guard down. I can't figure out why exactly, but the sudden emotional changes are intense. Try not to upset her too much.*"

"Roger," he said quietly and kept moving forward.

Before too long, they arrived at the foot of the towering twin buildings in front of the station. Perhaps because it was the weekend, the inside was packed with shoppers. They took the escalator up to the third floor, went into what appeared to be a stylish boutique, and began to examine the various items of clothing laid out there.

"*Come on, Shido. You can't just look,*" Kotori said impatiently.

His eyebrows jumped up, and he called out to Origami, who was patting the fur trim of a coat. "We came all the way here and everything. How about I buy you one thing as a present? What do you want?"

"What?" Her eyes grew round in surprise. "No, I couldn't. It's pretty expensive here. Look." She lowered her voice as she showed him the tag on the coat. 39,800 yen, an impossible price for a teenage boy.

But Shido had Ratatoskr for backup. He slapped a hand to his chest. "Not an issue."

"But—"

"In exchange, let me be the first person who sees you wearing it. That'll be my thank-you," he said, and Origami smiled bashfully.

"Itsuka, I bet you make all the girls cry."

"Huh? Wh-why...?"

"It's just, you seem pretty used to this," she said, rolling her eyes teasingly at him.

A bead of sweat rolled down his cheek. "H-hey, whoa..."

"Hee-hee!" Her face relaxed into a smile. "I'm kidding. Well, maybe I'll take you up on that offer. But since we're doing this, do you mind if I look around a bit more? If the condition is that I have to show you first, then I have to pick something that would make you happy."

"S-sure." Shido nodded, and Origami began to move around the store on light feet.

"Heh-heh-heh. Make all the girls cry." Kotori's voice echoed in his right ear. *"She sees right through you, Shido."*

"Lay off," he replied with a sigh.

"I'm not saying that's bad or anything. Of course, there's always the concern of becoming too slick with the ladies. But well, we don't have to worry about that with you, Shido."

"What's that supposed to mean?"

"That whiff of virgin that hangs about you—"

"Sorry. Actually, don't tell me." He covered his face with both hands, like he was weeping helplessly. He could hear Kotori sigh.

"Anyway, make sure you don't just leave Origami hanging."

"Oh. Right." He looked around. But Origami was nowhere to be seen. "Huh? Where'd she go?"

"And there we go. Reine, what's Origami's position?"

"...Mm. Approximately twenty meters behind Shin's position." He heard Reine's voice in response to Kotori. As Ratatoskr's analyst, she was also providing backup for him on *Fraxinus*.

"Sorry. Thanks," he said, turning around to walk those twenty meters. He discovered a changing room there, separated from the shop with a curtain.

"Oh, huh, okay. So that was it." He nodded in understanding. Made sense. No wonder he hadn't been able to see her. She had apparently picked something out and was trying it on. He looked at the items laid out on a nearby shelf to kill time until she came out.

"Eeeeaaaaah?!"

He heard her shriek suddenly inside the changing room and gasped. "Wh-what's wrong, Origami?!" he cried.

"Wh-why am I...?" He heard Origami's voice, colored with fear from the other side of the curtain.

He didn't have a good feeling about this. He set a hand on the curtain. "Sorry, Origami! I'm opening up!"

"Huh? Oh. N-no, don't, Itsuka—"

Ignoring her plea, he yanked the curtain open.

"Huh?" His jaw dropped when he saw her. That was only natural. Whatever else, Origami was slumped down helplessly on the floor of the changing room, wearing a school swimsuit, a headband with dog ears on her head, a dog tail accessory attached to her backside, and a leather collar around her neck. Most likely, anyone would have gaped for a second, at least.

"O-Origami? What are you...?" he started to say and then gasped, breaking out into a sweat. "You can't actually think the clothes I'd be happy with..."

Origami shook her head furiously. "D-don't get the wrong idea! I just... This is—!" She appeared confused, her eyes darting around, almost as if she herself didn't understand why she was in this getup. "I don't remember picking any of this stuff up, so how could I...?! Why a school swimsuit, of all things—?"

As she spoke, she grimaced like her head was suddenly hurting. "School swim... Dog ears... My head..." She pressed on the sides of her head, wincing in pain, and at the same time, Shido heard a beeping alarm through his earpiece.

"Shido! Origami's emotion levels!"

"O-Origami! Listen! How about you change, and we go someplace else for now? Okay?!" he cried, baffled, and closed the changing room curtain.

"...I'm sorry. After you invited me out and everything. I guess I'm a little off-kilter today," Origami said, pressing a hand to her forehead, sitting in a restaurant on the top floor of the same building about twenty minutes after they left the shop.

"Don't even worry about it. I asked you, so it's all good. If you're not really feeling great today, maybe we should call it a day early?" Shido asked, worried.

But Origami shook her head. "Mm-hmm. It's nothing like that. It's just..."

"Just?"

"It's nothing. At any rate, I'm okay," she said, as if to change the subject, and a smile rose on her face. "Sorry for making you worry."

His eyes were still on her, filled with concern, but maybe he decided to respect what she said. He didn't press her any further.

"..."

Origami let out a sigh so slight that Shido didn't notice it. It wasn't that walking around town with him was boring. In fact, it was so much fun, she could hardly stand it, to the point where she wondered when was the last time she'd been this excited. And yet she was overcome with a curious feeling.

She didn't know the reason herself, but when she saw the costume in the cosplay shop that was so striking she wondered when anyone would ever wear it, an urge from deep in the back of her mind had crashed over her like a wave. A feeling almost like she had once worn it herself.

Of course, there was no way. Never in her life had Origami put on such a lunatic outfit—school swimsuit, dog ears, dog tail, collar! Even if she were ordered at gunpoint to put on such a getup, it was so indecent that she would have hesitated for at least a second. Only a person with some screws loose would have happily worn something like this.

But that wasn't the only thing. It was the same when Shido had taken her to that sketchy store where they sold medicine. She'd grabbed a shopping basket half-unconsciously and tossed in bottles from the shelves in a fluid movement. She'd even frowned at the fact that she didn't have a point card for the store in her wallet.

"Have I...been there before?" she murmured to herself.

"Huh?" Shido looked up at her in confusion as the food they'd ordered was brought to the table.

She turned her eyes toward it, as if to deflect from what she'd just said. "Come on, Itsuka. Better eat before it gets cold?"

"Hmm? R-right." Urged on by Origami, Shido picked up a spoon and started in on his omurice.

Origami also reached out for her seafood doria.

When he'd finished about half his omurice, Shido abruptly pressed a hand to his right ear and stood. "Sorry. I need to go for a sec. I'll be back soon."

"Oh. Okay." What could have happened? But interrogating him would get her nowhere. She nodded quietly and watched him leave. And once he was completely out of her sight, she let out a long, loud sigh. "Haah. What is going on with me?"

Shido had been nice enough to ask her out, but with all her odd behavior, she felt like she needed to apologize to him. She had to get it together. She set her spoon down and pinched her cheeks to fire herself up.

"Ah."

Her eyes stopped on a certain something. Even though she had only just made up her mind to quit being so weird, she felt her heart twist up in her chest. The something, it was…

"I-Itsuka's…spoon…"

Yes. The fact that he'd left his seat in the middle of eating meant that his used spoon was just sitting there on the table.

She felt her heart pounding with incredible force.

"N-no, no, no. What am I even thinking…?"

She hurried to restrain the hand that was creeping forward. This was just too much, simply too much. If she did this, she would be a magnificent pervert. Straight to jail.

And yet her right hand pushed forward with incredible force. It felt almost like there was another Origami inside her who was making her move.

"Hngh! Calm down, hand," she tried saying, but her words had no effect.

The swirling vortex in her head began to pick up speed, and she no longer understood anything about this world. What was right anyway? What was wrong again? The standards of correct and incorrect were vague, changing with the times. Could her actions really be criticized at the end of the day? (Rhetorical question.) What did it mean to be wrong? If she failed to act in this moment, was that not actually defying the natural order of the universe? The philosopher Olearin Dovich once said it. No one can prove my existence, but the fact that I am licking Shido's spoon definitely exists. In other words, lickety *ergo sum*.

Her mind hazy, Origami felt the left hand holding her right hand back loosen its grip.

"Hey, sorry for making you wait, Origami—" Returning from the washroom, Shido stopped in front of the table.

The reason was simple. He had stumbled upon Origami with his spoon in her hand, tongue stretched out with the most lascivious expression on her face.

"O-Origami…?"

She gasped, as if only then noticing his presence. Her eyes shone with a strange light, like she was possessed, and a cold sweat beaded on her face. "N-no! This isn't… No!" she cried out in panic.

"O-oh, it's fine." He didn't know what it wasn't, but he went with it. "I'm used to it."

"Listen! This is really not what it looks like! R-right, it's, um! When you stood up, your spoon fell off the table! I was just picking it up!" she cried, almost pleading with him, and stood, making her chair clatter.

The shock of this movement made the glasses on the table rock, and one of them tipped over toward Shido. Water splashed onto the bottom of his shirt.

"Whoops." He looked down at himself.

"Ah! I-I'm so sorry. I was flustered and—," she cried.

"Ha-ha! It's no big deal. It'll dry soon enough," he said, as if to reassure the apologetic Origami. He tugged on the hem of his shirt and twisted it slightly to wring the water out. His belly button peeked out.

"…!"

Origami whipped her phone out of her pocket at lightning speed and in one flowing movement turned the lens toward his belly button, snapping several pictures in succession.

"Huh?" He opened his eyes wide in surprise.

"Ah!" For some reason, Origami looked equally surprised. It was almost as if her body had been moving against her own will.

"You have to believe me, Itsuka… I—I… My body just…!" she begged, her eyes filling with tears. But all the while, her finger was holding the shutter button down. "Why?! Whyyyyyyyyy?!"

The sound of her cry and the repeated noise of the camera shutter echoed through the late afternoon restaurant.

Chapter 10
Angel of the Starry Sky

The time was six thirty PM. Now that November was upon them, the days were shorter, and the town had already sunk into the darkness of evening. The air was chilly, belying the warmth of the day, and when Shido let out a sigh, he generated a faint white fog that then disappeared. A brisk breeze made the trees sway and the fallen leaves dance.

As these footsteps of winter echoed around them, Shido and Origami went to the park up on the plateau with a view of the city. It was very atmospheric, perfect for the end of a date, or so were the instructions from *Fraxinus*.

From the edge of the park, they could see any number of stars. Although it was amusing that there were many more electric lights glittering on the ground than stars hanging in the sky.

"I guess it's no surprise that it'd get a little chilly at this hour," Shido said, and Origami nodded slightly as she gazed at the night sky.

"Mm-hmm," she said, rubbing her hands together with a faint smile. "You forget because it's warm during the day, out in the sun. I kind of wish I'd brought some gloves."

She'd been all over the place that day, but she'd managed to pull herself back together somehow. Well, any number of times since lunch, she *had* turned the lens of her phone on him before she herself even knew it, sniffed at his neck, and made like she was pouring something into a cup he had just drunk from, even though she didn't have anything in her hands, but... He hadn't paid any of this too much attention.

From what she said, all of it had stemmed from something like her body moving by pure reflex. Shido realized that somewhere inside him, he was relieved that Origami was still actually Origami.

"Ha-ha! I guess so. Oh, right! How about we get some canned coffee or—," he started to say, and then he heard Kotori's voice in his right ear.

"*C'mon, Shido, that's not what you do. She said her hands were cold, yeah?*"

"..." He darted his eyes around helplessly for a minute silently before nodding firmly, as if he had made up his mind, and placed his hand on top of Origami's. Although it was shaking a little bit, maybe because of nerves, maybe because of the cold.

"Huh?!" For a moment, her eyes grew as wide as saucers in surprise. But she quickly realized what he was trying to do. Her cheeks flushed, and she hung her head a little.

"*Heh-heh. Looking good,*" Kotori said, approvingly. "*Likability's not bad, either. We just might be able to finish this off today. Feels like we just need another little push to seal the deal.*"

And then, as if in response to this, Reine's voice came through his earpiece.

"*...Mm-hmm. It seems there's one last thing stuck inside her. This reaction... It's close to anxiety. Likely her not knowing if Shin will accept her for who she is or not.*"

"*Anxiety, hmm? Well, she did do all that weird stuff today,*" Kotori said with a wry smile. "*But that just makes the whole thing easier. All you have to do is put her at ease, right?*"

"Well, yeah, I guess, but how am I supposed to do that?" Shido asked in a low voice, and Kotori snorted triumphantly.

"It's obvious. Origami's anxious because she doesn't know if you're okay with who she is, right? So then the quickest deal with that would be to put it into words, yeah?"

"Meaning..."

"Your only option is to tell her you love her."

He had more or less expected this, but still a bead of sweat trailed down his cheek. He recalled the time in the original world when he had told Origami he liked her. When he thought about it now, that had also been at Kotori's instruction under the pretext of training.

In fact, that had been what caused the Origami of the original world to come after him more aggressively. Would it be the same for this Origami?

As Shido wondered about this, Kotori's voice rang out in his ear, urging him on.

"What are you dawdling for? We'll never get another chance like this to seal the Spirit-hunting Devil, you know? If we let this moment slip away, the other Spirits could be injured before our next opportunity to seal her power rolls around."

"Unh..."

Kotori was exactly right. It was the height of faithlessness to whisper his love to her when he hadn't fully committed himself. But if he didn't lock her powers away here and now, other people might end up getting hurt. It might be Tohka and the others whose powers had already been sealed, or it might be an as yet unknown Spirit. It was even possible that it would be Origami herself.

He couldn't allow that to happen. He took a deep breath, and still holding her hand, he turned toward Origami. "Hey, Origami?"

"What is it, Itsuka?" She turned curious eyes on him.

"So...I need to tell you something," he said.

They stared into each other's eyes, and he felt his heart start to pound loudly.

Looking at her like this, he saw all over again how cute she was. The smoky bangs on her forehead. Clear eyes adorned with long lashes.

Cherry-pink lips that threatened to steal his heart at the mere touch of them. The thought flitted through his mind that the Shido of the original world was one lucky guy to have a girl like this fall for him.

But he couldn't bask in this emotion forever. He swallowed hard and opened his mouth to erase the anxiety lurking in her heart.

"The truth is...there's something I need to say to you, too, Itsuka," she said quietly, a second before he could get the words out.

"Something you need to say to me?" he asked in response, losing his moment to tell her how he felt.

Origami averted her eyes for a few seconds, hesitating before she said slowly, "You know how I was in the AST—the SDF's Anti-Spirit Task Force?"

"Uh-huh." He nodded. "I do."

"But I quit not too long ago," she continued.

"Uh-huh..." He'd already heard from Kotori that she had left the AST, but it would have been weird for him to know that. "You did? Is that because you started having this low blood sugar and blacking out?"

Origami lowered her eyes. "Mm-hmm. That's one reason. Stuff like that's fatal in a job where you're regularly handling weapons. But...I guess it was after I started having symptoms. I stopped really understanding."

"Understanding what?" he asked.

"It's the AST's job to defeat the Spirits that cause the spacequakes," she said. "But I started wondering if we were doing the right thing."

"Wha...?" He was at a loss for words. And of course he was. The Origami he knew hated the Spirits and lived only to destroy them.

Perhaps the fact that her parents hadn't been killed by a Spirit made a serious difference, or maybe she had started to feel that way after she became a Spirit, albeit without her knowing. He didn't know the specific reason for it, but he never dreamed he'd hear such words from her.

But seeing his reaction, she furrowed her brow apologetically. "I'm sorry. I know it was a Spirit who killed your older brother, Itsuka."

"Oh! You don't have to apologize!" he said.

"Huh...?" She looked as though she hadn't expected that from him. She likely never imagined him saying something like that after his brother—although it had actually been him—was killed.

"I don't think you're wrong at all for thinking like that," he continued. "I—I mean, my brother would say the same thing, I just know it!"

"Itsuka," she said in a shaky voice, and the look on her face said she was about to burst into tears at any second. Her shoulders shook. "Oh! I-I'm sorry... I... Why am I...?" She turned her face away.

He didn't dare push her any further. He simply gripped her hand in his even more tightly.

"...!"

He heard what sounded like fanfare over his earpiece.

"Dramatic increase in likability!"

"Points have reached the maximum!"

"...Hmm. This seems to have been the cause of her lingering anxiety."

And then he heard the voices of Reine and the other crew members. So that was it. Origami had apparently been worried about how Shido would feel about these new feelings budding in her toward the Spirits.

"All right! Looking good, Shido! Get in there and land the final blow!" Kotori said, giving him the go signal.

He felt a jubilant abandon. He grinned, still holding Origami's hand.

None of this changed the fact that this was his big chance. He worked to get his breathing under control and calm the nervous pounding of his heart before turning quietly to Origami.

"So like—," he started to say.

"Oh! Itsuka, look!"

But he was interrupted for a second time in his attempt to tell her his feelings. Origami leaned forward over the wooden railing around the edges of the park and pointed up at the sky where a glittering star raced across it.

"A falling star! Look!" she cried. "We have to make a wish."

"Huh? But I mean, I don't know what to..." But even as he spoke, he was drawing up a wish in his mind. *Please let me seal Origami's Spirit*

powers properly. And, *please let Origami and the other Spirits get along.*
Although by that time, the star had basically disappeared from sight.

"...?"

As she looked up at the sky, leaning over the railing, Origami
abruptly gasped, and her hand, clutched in his, suddenly yanked him
forward.

"*Shido!*" Kotori's voice was like a warning in his right ear.

For a second, he didn't know what had happened. But he quickly
realized that the part of the railing bearing Origami's weight had
crumbled away with a cracking sound, maybe because it was old and
worn-out.

Naturally, Origami, pressed up against it, joined the railing in drop-
ping down, as if shoved off the edge of the park positioned high up on
the plateau.

"Eeaah?!" she screamed.

"Whoa!" he yelped in surprise.

But perhaps the silver lining was that he was still holding on to her
hand. He felt a jolt in his shoulder, and his arm stretched out at the
sudden load, but he managed to tighten his grip and yank Origami up.
He felt a sharp pain in his left hand, maybe because it had caught on
the cross-section of the broken railing.

"Hnnyaaag!" With a strange cry, he fell backward with Origami.

She let out a brief cry and landed on top of him as he lay flat on his
back.

"Owww," he groaned. "Y-you okay, Origami?"

"Y-yeah. Thanks, Itsuka," she replied, voice shaking. She must've
been quite stunned—he could feel her heart pounding fiercely through
her chest.

And then he realized that they were pressed so closely together that
he could tell how she was breathing.

"...!"

"*This is your chance, Shido! Likability's good. Do this!*" He heard
Kotori say.

And indeed, Origami's face was so close, he could have touched his lips to hers if he raised his head the tiniest bit. And given that they'd just escaped from certain doom, there was no better opportunity.

"Origami..." But right when he moved to kiss her, he noticed a change in her.

Her gaze was not on his face, but rather further down. At his left hand.

Following her eyes, Shido turned his gaze toward his hand and gasped. He'd cut himself open when he'd yanked Origami up, and the flames of Spirit power were flickering on that wound, licking at it.

Instantly, an earsplitting siren began to blare in his right ear.

"...!! *Shido! Run!*"

At the same time as Kotori's cry pierced his eardrum, Origami staggered to her feet from where she lay draped across him, as though pulled up by strings stretching down from the heavens. And when she was standing tall, she murmured with empty eyes, a totally changed person from before, "Spirit..."

"...!" His eyes flew open.

This was the exactly the same thing he'd seen on the school roof the other day when Origami saw the Spirit Kurumi.

Reine's hypothesis flitted through the back of his mind. Origami regained her memories of the original world only when she saw a Spirit, which was when she transformed into a Spirit. And the flames licking at his arm were none other than the power of the Spirit Efreet.

"Ah. Ah. Aaah. Ah. Ah. Aaaah." Origami looked up at the sky with those same empty eyes as her whole body began to spasm. Saliva hung from the corners of her mouth, and her posture was clearly abnormal.

"O-Origami, stop—," Shido called out to her, stunned. But before he could finish speaking, an intense veil of Spirit power rose around her body, and he was easily knocked backward.

"Hngh?!"

Even as he hit the ground on his back, he somehow softened his fall and crawled forward as he yanked his head up.

A jet-black spiderweb was shooting out, a circle with Origami at its center, swirling around her like a tornado.

"That's..." He gasped.

Ebony Astral Dress, like mourning clothes. This was without a doubt the inverted Spirit that had destroyed the Tengu of his original world.

"Mm." In one unit of the Spirit apartment building, Tohka was rolling around on the sofa, clutching a large cushion to her chest.

It wasn't only her in the apartment at that moment. When she turned her eyes toward the TV, she saw the Yamai sisters competing in a racing game with a popsicle on the line, and behind them, she caught sight of Yoshino and Natsumi chatting happily. Because Shido and Kotori had some big something that day, there was no one home at the Itsuka house, so they had all gathered together in Tohka's apartment.

"Mmm." She hummed for the millionth time and rolled over on the sofa. It wasn't that she was particularly upset about nobody being home. This had happened any number of times before. It was true that she was a little sad she didn't get to eat Shido's cooking, but he and Kotori were both busy, so Tohka couldn't exactly go making trouble for them with her own little selfish desires.

But it was strange. For some reason, she felt weirdly off-balance that day. And actually, it wasn't just today. For a few days now, ever since that new student had transferred into their class, she'd felt this weird itchiness in her heart that she could barely stand.

When she made her complicated noise of displeasure, Miku peered at her from where she sat leaning back against the sofa. "Hee-hee-hee! What's the maaaatter, Tohka? Are you all out of sorts because Daaarling's not here?"

"It's not that. It's just..." Tohka grimaced and set her thoughts in search of the words that would express her current feelings. But she couldn't come up with any particularly good turns of phrase. "Mm."

"Aah." Miku's cheeks turned red as her face relaxed into a smile, and she leaped over the sofa with the grace of an athlete jumping over a high hurdle, to slide herself between Tohka and the sofa back.

"Oooh, you! That look on your face is sending me! Ooh-hoo! Ooh-hoo!" she said, twisting herself about. That latter noise was the sound of her pressing her face to Tohka's back and panting wildly.

"What are you doing, Miku?!" Tohka cried. "You're tickling me!"

"Mm-hmm, it's all gooood! It's not like it'll cost you anythiiiing." Miku slipped her arms around Tohka and passionately pressed her cheek to the other girl's.

Tohka put a hand on Miku's forehead, pushed her hard, and tried to pry her off.

"…?!" And then she frowned unconsciously. She didn't totally know why. But she felt something suddenly, a sensation like sparks flying in her head.

"Wha…?"

"Shiver. What was that—?"

It seemed that she was not the only one to feel it. The Yamai sisters both lifted their faces in the middle of their competition. Perhaps they'd messed up while playing their game—the TV showed cars crashing.

Farther behind them, Yoshino and Natsumi also frowned and looked around, while Miku, clinging to Tohka, also got a surprised look on her face.

"Wh-what was that?" she breathed.

"…"

Instinctively sensing danger, Tohka leaped off of the sofa, opened the window, and stepped onto the balcony of the apartment in her bare feet. She leaned over the railing and looked both ways to find a faint light coming from near the plateau off in the distance in the night sky.

"There…!"

The light was not bright enough for the average person to have paid it any mind. But the Spirit Tohka immediately realized that this shining was due to Spirit power. And that there was someone in that place with incredible power.

"Hmph. Incredibly dubious. This feeling…"

"Assent. That is…a Spirit."

The Yamai sisters and the other girls followed Tohka onto the balcony. And as if on some kind of cue, they turned their eyes in the direction where Tohka had sensed the Spirit power.

"Um." Yoshino pointed tentatively. "Over there."

"Ohh, isn't there a park in that area?" Miku said.

"…!"

The absent Shido's face popped up in Tohka's head.

Right. Now that she was thinking about it, Shido had taken her to that spot once before. As soon as she made this connection, her heart started pounding like an alarm bell.

It wasn't as though she knew for a fact that Shido was up there. But in the back of her mind, his face mixed with the sense of oddness that had been hanging over her for the last few days, making her pulse race.

"Tohka?!"

"Tohka!"

"…!"

The other girls cried as, half-unconsciously, Tohka stepped onto the balcony railing and leaped off into the night.

"*Spirit power, category E! Origami Tobiichi has inverted!*"

"*Ngh! So Reine's hypothesis was right!*"

Through the earpiece in his right ear, Shido heard the voices of Kotori and her crew, along with an endless alarm that instinctively called up danger.

"…"

As he listened to all this commotion, he looked up alone, quietly, at the figure of Origami. Naturally, he was confused. Just when he thought he'd finally saved her, she had inverted once again, sending powerful shivers of fear down his spine. But in the midst of all this, somewhere in his head, he was able to assess the situation with absolute calm.

Shido turned toward Origami and kicked at the ground. But before he could reach her, the wall of Spirit power spinning around her sent him flying once again.

"Ngh!" he groaned.

"*Shido!*" Kotori yelled. "*What are you doing?!*"

"If I don't stop Origami now, things are going to get really bad!"

Yes. If her inversion was due to the fact that she'd seen the healing flames he'd generated unconsciously, then her inversion would not stop until her target—Shido—had been eliminated. But naturally, he couldn't create a body double the way Kurumi had. Meaning Origami would rampage until he died. If the condition of quelling her inversion was fulfilled, in exchange they would forever lose the means of sealing her Spirit powers.

Of course, Shido had the power of the healing flames given to him by Kotori. Any superficial wounds would be healed where he stood. But there was a limit to this. He had indeed taken the place of Origami's parents five years earlier, but he didn't know if his body had actually healed itself with Kotori's Spirit power, or if the time limit on Yud Bet had run out immediately before the beam of light hit him.

And assuming that it *was* possible for him to heal that sort of damage, it was also quite possible that Origami would remain inverted for as long as she perceived him to be alive. In which case, now was his only chance. His only opportunity to get close to her was when she hadn't manifested those feathers.

"Origami!" he yelled as he recalled the sight he'd previously witnessed. The inverted Origami raining darkness down from the heavens, running rampant over the city. He couldn't let that happen again. He couldn't let Origami do that again.

He clenched his hands into fists and was about to charge at Origami once more.

"*Stop, Shido! Get away from Origami right now!*" Kotori's voice rang out in his ear, and he stopped automatically.

"Wh-what are you talking about?!" he cried. "This is our only—"

"*I told you to get away from her. You planning to break through a wall of Spirit power with your bare fists?*"

"Huh?" His eyes grew wide in surprise.

At the same time as he heard Kotori's voice, he saw several pale lights appear around Origami, and in the blink of an eye, they turned into chunks of sharp metal. Pieces shaped like diamonds stretched out on one side. If he had to say, the objects looked almost like enormous leaves. They deployed an invisible wall around him and turned their tips to encircle Origami.

"What the...?" He stared, stunned.

"*Yggdrafolium, activate!*"

The instant Kotori gave this command, the leaves' invisible wall grew larger and closed in to restrain Origami, draped in her inky-black Astral Dress, crushing her from all directions.

"Wh—?"

"*Yggdrafolium,*" Kotori said with a little sniff. "*Fraxinus's all-purpose autonomous units, each deploying its own Territory, took the liberty of setting it up around the two of you. I never dreamed we'd actually end up using it, though.*"

In the next instant, he spotted a momentary flash in the sky far above the park, and then the airship *Fraxinus* appeared before him as if the mirrored surface around it had been peeled away. It had at some point descended to a position where it was visible to the naked eye.

Normally, *Fraxinus* used Realizers to deploy camouflage that made it invisible. The distant ship only revealed itself when the Realizers were working in places beyond the Territory deployed around the ship—more specifically, only when recovering people or materials from the outside using the transporter or when sending Yggdrafolium out into the world. Or when they were firing the main armament Mistilteinn.

"Kotori, you're not actually...?!" Shido cried, and as if in response, *Fraxinus* slowly dipped forward in the sky and turned its weapons on

Origami on the ground. It was an extremely unstable position that would have been impossible to maintain for anything other than an airship controlled using a Territory.

And then the barrels of the guns flashed with magical light.

"Relax. *We're not going full blast here*," Kotori told him. "*Mistilteinn'll break down the Spirit power wall for a few seconds, so get in there when it does!*"

"…! R-right!" he cried.

"*I don't want to rough her up, but we can't let her destroy the city, either.*"

"*Commander, magic is fully charged. Ready to fire on your word!*" A crew member's voice rang out.

"*Excellent. Target—Origami Tobiichi on the ground! Don't you go missing her, Kannazuki!*"

"*Not to worry.*" The calm voice of *Fraxinus* Vice Commander Kyouhei Kannazuki echoed in Shido's ear.

"*Mistilteinn, f—*"

"Kotori! Get out of heeeeere!" he shouted so loudly that his throat nearly started bleeding.

The reason was simple. Just like the Yggdrafolium encircling Origami on the ground, feathers emitting a jet-black light—Satan—had popped into being around *Fraxinus* floating in the dark sky.

"*Huh?*"

He heard the stunned voice of Kotori and an alarm warning of danger through his earpiece.

Satan turned toward *Fraxinus*, and every feather shot beams of black light at it, like concentrated darkness. The white body of the airship was showered, exploded, disappeared, pierced in black from all directions. Shido heard the explosions and the cries of Kotori and her crew in his right ear.

"*Eeeaaah!*"

"Kotori! Kotori?!" he cried, but he got no reply.

Smoke spewed forth from the airship hanging in the sky, while the Yggdrafolium restraining Origami flickered and dropped to the ground lifelessly.

"Ah." His eyes grew wide in fear, and he let out a short cry.

Fraxinus was plummeting from the night sky. The sight was almost exactly the same as the scene he had witnessed in the original world. At that time, too, *Fraxinus* had been downed by Origami.

"Why…? Why?!" he shouted half-unconsciously.

The history he had supposedly changed, the world he'd supposedly overwritten was changing bit by bit to converge with the original series of events. It almost felt like the universe was telling him that no matter how he struggled and fought, the result that had already been determined could never be changed.

"…"

Freed from her bonds, Origami floated up into the air without a word as she curled into herself like a fetus, almost like she was closing her mind off from the outside world. At the same time, the tips of those innumerable feathers shone with darkness, as if for a follow-up attack on *Fraxinus* as it slowly lost altitude.

"…! Origami!" Shido called and tried to run to her once more. But he was repelled by a wall of Spirit power, and he couldn't come close to her while the black feathers hanging in the sky were on the verge of launching an attack against *Fraxinus*.

The airship had already been half-destroyed in the earlier attack. If it took another hit now, he had no idea what would happen to the ship and the crew inside it.

"Stop, Origami! You have to stopppppp!"

But his cry didn't reach her.

Beams of inky light shot forth from the dark feathers.

"…!!"

And then wind abruptly began to gust from out of nowhere, rocking the black feathers and changing their direction ever so slightly. Satan's light grazed *Fraxinus*, stretched out into the night sky, and disappeared.

However powerful the wind pressure might have been, though, a mere gust could not have disturbed Satan. Shido realized the true nature of this wind and gasped. "It's…"

In the next instant, several small feathers manifested around Origami's body, and in the blink of an eye, they turned toward Shido. Apparently, he had also been judged to be an enemy.

"Ngh?!" He wouldn't be able to escape from this many of them. He stiffened, bracing himself for the impact to come.

But a second before the feathers of Origami's Angel could fire, he heard a cry from the sky above.

"Haaaaah!"

A Spirit manifesting a limited Astral Dress was swinging a massive sword and knocking the black feathers flying.

"You okay, Shido?!"

"Tohka!" He called the girl's name. Yes. The person who had appeared there was Tohka, who was supposed to be in the apartment building next door to the Itsuka house.

And it wasn't just her. Looking like they had been chasing after her, Spirits began to appear one after the other in the park, all clad in limited Astral Dresses. Yoshino on the back of an enormous rabbit puppet, Natsumi in grown-up form, Miku materializing a keyboard of light around her body. And in the sky, the Yamai sisters who had called up that gust of wind and saved *Fraxinus* in a tight spot.

"What…? What are you all doing here?!" he cried.

"Uh. U-um," Natsumi stammered.

"Hee-hee-hee!" Miku giggled. "It's oooobvious that we would come running when you're in trouble, Daaarling!"

"Well, we mostly just followed Tohka."

"Ooh! You can't say *that* paaart!"

Miku held a shushing finger to her lips. Grown-up Natsumi shrugged with a nonchalance that was completely different from her usual form.

"Anyway, Shido." Tohka brandished her Angel Sandalphon to protect Shido from further attack and glared at Origami, not letting her guard down. "I sense incredible Spirit power. Who exactly *is* that?"

He clenched his hands into such tight fists that his nails cut into his palms as he replied, "That's…Origami."

"What...? That's the transfer student?" Tohka said dubiously. But that was only natural. The Tohka of this world had only just come into contact with Origami. And above all else, no one was going to simply nod and accept that a person floating in the air in a jet-black Astral Dress was their classmate. Not this overwhelming majesty that made a person shrink in fear simply facing it.

DEM's Isaac Westcott had called an inverted Spirit the Demon King, and this before Shido's eyes now was filled with such an immense power that the expression was no exaggeration.

"...!"

However. Shido gritted his teeth and took a step forward.

"Shido?" Tohka furrowed her brow. Most likely, she wanted to tell him it was dangerous. And he was only all too well aware of that. But he had to reach Origami.

If he left her free like this, up in the sky, the city of Tengu before his eyes would once again transform into ruins, like in his memory. And Origami would never again be Origami. That alone he had to prevent at all costs. And while the possibility was extremely slim, the only one who could take her hand was Shido.

But his power alone wouldn't be enough. Before the immensely powerful Demon King, he was simply too weak.

"Gang," he said to the Spirits coming together around him.

Maybe he should have told them to run. Said not to fight Origami. But even as he apologized to them in his mind, he could only say, "Help me...to help her!"

Standing before him, Tohka looked blankly at him for a second before replying, "What are you talking about? Of course we will." She tightened her grip on Sandalphon. "You saved me, Shido. You taught me about the beauty of the world. You created my world. So now it's my turn to help you."

"Tohka..." He didn't know what to say.

The other Spirits also nodded and chimed in one after the other.

"Me and Yoshinon... We want to help you!"

"Yes, exactly. You just be a good boy and let the ladies take care of this. You're not so tough, Shido. You can't go overdoing it!"

"And if you had told us to run away, well, you may be my darling, but I would be soooo angry?"

Yoshino, Natsumi, and Miku weighed in with grins. And then the laughing voices of Kaguya and Yuzuru dancing in the air echoed through the area.

"Kah-kah! Excellent! We have heard your call! The children of the hurricane, the Yamais shall lend you their strength!"

"Contract. Please let Yuzuru and Kaguya handle things in the air."

"Thanks, you guys." Shido tightened his hands into fists. "Now let's go. To Origami."

Origami was perplexed.

Shido had caught her when she nearly fell off the edge of the park, and then she'd seen some kind of flickering light on his arm, and her consciousness had faded again, just like always.

When she came to, she was standing in an unfamiliar place. It was a white space with nothing as far as the eye could see. She didn't even know if it was the sky or a ceiling above her head, or if there was level ground before her. She was, at any rate, "standing" in this place, but even the earth pressing up under her feet felt less than solid, and she was overcome by the misapprehension that she might float up into the air if she let her guard down. It felt almost like she had wandered into a blank manga panel.

"*What is this place?*" she murmured absently, looking around. "*This has to be a dream…right?*"

It didn't take too long for her to make this decision. But that was really no wonder. There was no way a space like this could exist in reality.

"*Huh…?*" Her eyes flew open abruptly.

Ahead of her, in the space where there had been nothing before, a girl had appeared. She had a slender physique, which was clothed in a dress as black as night. She was curled up into herself, holding her knees, an empty look on her face.

"*Who are—?*" she started to say and then realized something with a gasp. "*Is that...me?*"

Yes. It hadn't connected at first because of the seeming impossibility, but no matter how she looked at it, this girl was *her*.

No, actually. That wasn't quite right. In contrast with Origami's own hair, which hung halfway down her back, the hair of the girl curled up in front of her was barely long enough to tickle her shoulders. Simply put, the only other notable difference was the clothes she was wearing. A cold sweat beaded on Origami's forehead at the curious, out-of-place sensation of looking in a mirror.

"*What even is this?*" She couldn't help but furrow her brow, despite the fact that she'd already decided that this place and this feeling were a dream.

But in that instant, unfamiliar scenes and words poured into her mind.

"*...!*"

Although they weren't entirely unfamiliar, somehow. As she instantaneously acquired this vast sea of information, she felt a growing certainty inside her.

"*These are...my memories?*"

Yes. She was seeing several years' worth of memories, experiences she would have had if she'd walked a slightly different path.

Origami closed her mind.

The information that opened within her in the moment she witnessed the Spirit power flames were the memories of the Origami of the original world that she had forgotten. As they ate into her consciousness, she felt her body and her mind dyed a pure black.

Five years earlier. Yes, that summer day five years ago, it had been her parents who were killed before her eyes. And the Spirit who had killed them was Origami herself.

The second she remembered this, Origami lost any ability to think about anything at all. This might have been a defensive instinct, a desire to protect herself.

The fundamental element that had shaped her up to this point, the meaning of her life, her purpose for existing.

Realizing that these had returned from nothing in the worst possible form, her brain had separated the Origami of this world from those memories so that her sense of self would not be completely destroyed. This was the rule in this world. The moment Spirit power manifested in the Origami of this world, her consciousness split, and control of her body was ceded to the Origami with intact memories of the original world.

Now, Origami thought nothing. Believed nothing. Felt nothing. Her strength was turned to one thing alone—killing the Spirit before her eyes.

However, a small light abruptly appeared inside the head of the Origami who had supposedly abandoned everything. She didn't know what had happened. And even if she had known, the Origami of that moment couldn't be aware of it.

Or she shouldn't have been.

But that light expanded into a certain memory inside her head. Yes. It was the memory of the Origami who lived in the world where her parents hadn't died that day five years earlier.

"...*Ah...*," she said softly.

At the same time, the minds of Origami and *Origami* began to mix, blending into each other.

"Kah-kah! We are the beloveds of the wind, children of the hurricane!"

"Concord. There isn't anyone in this world who can keep up with us."

The Yamai sisters kicked at the air in perfect sync with each other and danced lightly up into space. In the next instant, beams of light shot through the spot where they had only just been. It seemed that after attacking *Fraxinus*, Satan now perceived the two of them as a threat.

"Hmph! However powerful your might, it is all for naught if you cannot land any hits!" Kaguya declared as she dodged the incoming beams by a hair with deft mid-flight acrobatics.

"Counsel. It is time, Shido," Yuzuru said to Shido on the ground, as she evaded the shots in the same way as Kaguya. "Reach the main body while Yuzuru and Kaguya are drawing its fire."

He nodded firmly and turned his gaze back to Origami. "Let's do this, gang!" he cried.

"Yeah!" the Spirits replied as one.

But at the same time, Origami, free of Yggdrafolium's restraint, was slowly ascending into the air. He couldn't let her escape into the sky.

"Miku!" he called.

"Yes, yeeessss! Allow me!" Miku slid her fingers across the keyboard of light deployed around her and began to play a flowing melody. "Gabriel. Rondo!"

A number of silver pipes appeared around Origami, the ends turned toward her. The notes Miku played had a power that wasn't visible to the eye, and these layered upon each other to press Origami to the ground as she tried to rise.

"Hee-hee! Look at you go, Miku!" Natsumi laughed bewitchingly. "But while you're holding this girl down, you can't do your original job, hmmm? In that case..."

Natsumi brandished her right hand to manifest an Angel that looked like a broom. "Haniel. Kaleidoscope."

The broom she clutched twisted like it was made of soft clay and reformed itself into a silver pipe and keyboard.

"Huh?! That's—!" Miku stared, baffled as she played her song. And of course she did. Natsumi had manifested an Angel in the exact same form as that of her own Gabriel.

"I'm just gonna borrow it a sec, hon. Truth is, ever since I saw it, I've wanted to try copying it," Natsumi said as she crossed her arms in front of her and hit the keyboard hard. An intense etude filled the air. "March!"

As the song reached their ears, Shido and the others felt strength welling up inside themselves. Although there was a slight difference in the sound, this was without a doubt Miku's March.

"Oooh!" Miku squealed. "You little copycat!"

"Heh-heh." Natsumi chuckled. "No big, right? It's for Shido and all."

"Boo. You're going to pay the proper copyright license fee later, you knoooow. Rights in the idol world are veeeery strict!" Miku puffed up her cheeks in a pout. It seemed she was vexed that hers was the only Angel that Natsumi had re-created. That said, however, the fact that Gabriel now existed both offensively and defensively was a great source of strength for them. Tohka and Yoshino leaned forward, ready to charge Origami.

But almost as if in resistance to their renewed determination, the air around Origami distorted to produce even more of the Angel's feathers. These flew around in irregular orbits, firing light beams at Shido and the Spirits.

"Ngh!"

"Shido!"

"Hup!"

Yoshino and Yoshinon—transformed into her Angel Zadkiel—shot forward to protect Shido. The moisture in the air concentrated and instantly froze to knock Origami's beams off course.

"Thanks, Yoshino, Yoshinon!" he cried. "Just in the nick of time!"

"Mm-hmm… But please watch out. They're coming again!" Yoshino said, eyeing the feathers dancing in the sky cautiously.

A myriad of little feathers floated around Origami. It would have been a different story if the Spirits had manifested their complete Astral Dresses, but in their current limited Astral Dresses, even a single blow might prove fatal. The Yamai sisters and Yoshino had deftly dodged or deflected Origami's attacks, but they couldn't keep that up forever. Shido had to get to Origami somehow, and soon.

As his thoughts raced, the tips of the feathers turned as one toward him, almost like they had detected his intentions.

"Hah!"

He heard a fierce battle cry, light flashed in front of him, and the feathers were all sent flying.

"Tohka!" he shouted. Yes. With a single blow from Sandalphon, she had attacked the feathers before they could fire on him.

But Sandalphon's limited power couldn't actually destroy the feathers. They began to move, as though they each had their own individual will, and darkness bloomed at their tips once more.

"Yoshino, back Shido up!" Tohka cried, her back toward him.

"O-okay…!" Yoshino replied and dressed the front of Zadkiel in icy air like armor. "Let's go, Shido! Please get behind me!"

"R-right!" he cried.

She pulled back both hands like she was pulling the strings of a marionette and made Zadkiel advance. Shido hid behind the massive rabbit and followed it toward Origami.

But mere seconds later, Zadkiel came to a halt. When Shido peeked around it, he saw that new feathers had manifested around Origami, creating a powerful wall of Spirit power. When the feathers attacked him, all he and the Spirits had to do was knock them off course. But when they drilled down on defense like this, his band of fighters had no choice but to push past with force.

"Unh… Unnnnh!" Yoshino groaned.

"Hngaaah! This thing's hard as rock!" Yoshinon shouted.

"Yoshino! Yoshinon!" Shido called. "You okay?!"

"We're…okay!" Yoshino returned, sounding pained. She definitely didn't sound okay. But then her gaze sharpened, and she clenched her hands so that Zadkiel curled up into a ball. "I'm…a scaredy-cat…and a crybaby… But if it'll help you reach her…"

Zadkiel began to shine faintly.

"I need…the power to break through the wall." Yoshino splayed her fingers, and the strings stretching from her hands to Zadkiel's back glittered. "Zadkiel… Shiryon!"

Instantly, Zadkiel's massive bulk began to twist and distort, and before Shido knew it, it was coalescing into the strings connected with Yoshino's fingers. And then the brightly shining strings began to curl and wind themselves around Yoshino.

"Yoshino?!" Shido cried out at this unfamiliar sight.

But the response he got was…

"Yes, Shido." Her voice was firm now, and he could hear a new note of determination in it.

The light subsided, and he could finally see her again.

"Armor…?" he murmured, dazed.

Yes. Yoshino now stood before him clad in silver armor. Actually, he wasn't entirely sure whether it could really be called armor. The material it was made of was neither metal nor plastic, and this had become one with transparent ice to cover Yoshino over her Astral Dress. It looked almost like she was wearing Zadkiel.

"Mm…!" She wrapped icy air around her body, thrust both hands forward, and twined her fingers together. A snowstorm spiraled up from her silver arms and formed an enormous cone.

"Aaaaaaah…!" She yanked her clasped hands around. The auger of icy air around her hands moved like a drill to wrench an opening between feather and feather.

"Shido…!" she cried. "Now…!"

"R-right!" Shido called back and dived through the opening she had created for him. He raced toward Origami.

Held back by Miku's Rondo, Origami had stopped her ascent in a position about a meter from the ground. Naturally, with her inverted power, she could have easily repelled the music of Miku, who could only command a limited amount of her former power. But Shido couldn't sense anything like vitality or will in the girl before him.

It was only the inky-black feathers attacking; Origami herself hadn't so much as said a word. It was almost like a body's immune function eliminating external enemies regardless of the will of the person.

"Origami!" He shouted her name.

But she didn't even twitch in response. Eyes colored with despair looked blankly out into empty space.

"Ngh!" He gritted his teeth, remembering the scene in the original world.

Then, too, he had made it to Origami with the help of the Spirits, just like now. But Origami's mind had been completely closed off, and she hadn't reacted to anything he said. The exact same thing was happening all over again.

His own power alone wasn't enough. He needed something else, something he hadn't had then. He raised his voice. He stretched out his hand. What he needed now was a shock from within Origami that would make her take that hand.

Inside Origami's head, two sets of memories were blending together. It was a strange sensation, like she was looking at another her inside herself from both perspectives simultaneously.

And she was. The Origami of the original world and the Origami of this world were both Origami. Now that this Origami had both sets of memories in her head, she understood everything.

The bizarre disconnect she'd felt on the date with Shido today. The feeling of her body moving like it had a mind of its own. These both came out of a latent consciousness inside her, reacting to Shido's presence.

This situation was the same. Normally, the Origami of this world would not have been awake when her Spirit powers were manifesting. But due to the influence of Shido, the boundary between her memories of this world and that world had blurred, resulting in this irregularity of Origami's two sets of memories coming into contact.

This brought about a kind of chaos inside her. The Origami who closed her mind and tried to discard everything and the Origami who was trying to stop that somehow were tangled together in complicated ways inside a single vessel.

"Five years ago, I killed—"

"That never happened in this world! Itsuka's older brother saved Mom and Dad five years ago!"

She saw in her mind the face of the boy who had sacrificed himself for her parents. She realized abruptly that it hadn't been Shido's older brother—it had been Shido himself. Now that she had her memories of the original world, she was sure of it.

And then the sweet year she'd spent with her parents after the fire unfolded in her mind. Her mother and father, smiling. Their warm, happy family. The priceless time the three of them had spent together.

If only she'd had *these* memories. If these images had remained in the back of her mind, Origami would have certainly led a different life.

However.

"So…what is this, then? What are *these memories inside me?!"*

The world around her was on fire. She saw the city burning in her head. The crater dug out of the street. The scattered body parts. The scorched blood that hadn't even had the chance to flow. Her younger self looking up into the sky. This was evidently what the Origami of the original world had experienced that day five years earlier.

She was overwhelmed with nausea while the hellish memories rocked her to her core.

"Unh. Ah… Ah…"

The vividness of it all. And of course it was vivid. Because it was none other than Origami herself who had experienced it.

"I… I can't… It's…too…"

"The…horror…"

Nearly crushed by a mixture of grief, rage, and an incredible self-loathing, Origami tried to cry out.

But another memory came floating up, stopping her cold.

An event in the original world she could have no way of knowing about. An inverted field of view. Darkness spreading across the sky. A destroyed city. The sight was so ghastly that she nearly screamed.

"Ah. Ah. Ah. Aaaaaaah…!"

It wasn't happening in this world. But she herself had definitely made it happen in another one. She felt her field of view shudder and warp. She could barely stay conscious as the memories tried to paint her very existence black. But she had to. If she lost consciousness, there would no longer be anyone who could stop her.

Just because the awful events of five years ago had been "erased," that didn't mean she could shrug her shoulders and walk away from it now. Just because the large-scale destruction that crushed the original world wasn't happening here, it didn't mean that she could avert her eyes and forget about it.

If she gave up now, she would end up repeating her original actions in this world, where she hadn't done anything yet. Cities would fall. People would die. And if that happened, then Origami was sure she would never come back from that. She had to prevent this at least, whatever it took.

But.

"Unh... Ah. Aaah!"

The stream of negative emotions flooding into her brought her to her knees at last. She knew, though. She knew that the mistakes she'd made didn't exist in this world. That she could do things over in this world. Because while she now shared these memories of the original world, she also had her memories of *this* world.

But even as she recognized these facts, she was also half-broken by the certainty that she could not be allowed to continue living, that her crimes were too great for that.

"St...op. I... Ah. Aaaaaaaaaah...!" she shrieked.

But her voice alone wasn't enough. The Origami of this world couldn't save the Origami of the original world by herself. The most she could do was share her memories of this world and open Origami's eyes.

Yes. All Origami could do was give Origami a push. To save Origami, someone from outside would have to call out to her. Someone would have to take her hand.

But who would reach out to an inverted Origami sowing despair in the world—?

✳　　✳　　✳

"…Origami…?"

"…!" She lifted her face at the abrupt echo of her name. "*Shi…do…*"

Yes. The voice ringing out in this blank nothingness was none other than that of Shido Itsuka.

Krrrk. A crack appeared in the snowy-white space.

"*How…?*" Her own voice certainly didn't reach him.

But Shido raised his voice and kept speaking. As if calling out to her. "Don't try to carry it all by yourself! I told you five years ago, didn't I?! You're not alone!"

"*Ah…*" His words called up a memory inside her.

I'll take on your sadness! I'll shoulder your anger! When you're lost, you can lean on me! Use me when you're at the end of your rope! You can hit me with everything and then some! So! So…!

"*Ah. Aaah…*"

"Just don't give in to despair!" The voices of the Shido in her memory and the Shido calling to her now blended together, and she felt the cracks in the space around her grow even bigger.

"No matter how many worlds you try to destroy, I'll always show up and sort it out! No matter how many times you're on the verge of despair, I will always save you!"

"*I…*"

"So reach out your hand! I…I *need* you!"

"*…*"

The instant she heard those words, Origami felt her body move separately from her own will.

Now that she was thinking about it, this was very similar to the curious sensation from her date in this world with Shido today. The memories of the Origami from the original world had been making the body of the Origami of this world move.

However, now, unlike before, it was the memories of the Origami in *this* world reaching Origami's hand out toward Shido. Almost like they were telling her to live.

The empty space cracked and shattered.

"Shi...do..." Origami had been still like a corpse, but now a faint light flickered in her eyes. Shido's own eyes flew open in surprise.

"...! Origami!!" he cried.

After slowly looking around to take in her surroundings, she opened trembling lips. "I—I...," she said in a strangled voice.

"...!" He wrapped his arms around her. Just like he had that day five years earlier.

"Shido..." She continued mumbling quietly. "Thank...you, Shido. For...calling me."

"Origami—"

"If you hadn't been here... I almost did something I could never take back again." Tears spilled from her eyes and dampened his shoulder with their heat. "I... I can't erase the fact that I killed my mother and father... Or the crime of killing all those people in the original world... That will never, ever go away. Even if you made it like it never happened."

"...! That's—" *Not true.* But he couldn't bring himself to say something so mindless.

Events that hadn't happened in this world. A tragedy that most likely no one else remembered. Facts that Shido had effectively undone.

He gritted his teeth and half groaned. "I know," he said. "That's something you'll have to carry with you."

This was the cruelest declaration. Maybe he had no right to say it. Although he had done it to save so many lives, revising history was without a doubt a crime in its own right.

But he couldn't lie to her. He felt that conjuring up some pretty words, pretending he thought something other than what he did would have been a preposterous dishonoring of Origami's parents, the people of the city, and the Origami of the original world.

"I... I was..." Origami shuddered. "Ah. Waah... Aaaaaaah! Aaaaaa-aaaaaaah!"

She clung to Shido and began to weep loudly. Just like she had that day five years earlier.

Yes. He had no doubt that after entrusting her tears to him that day, she had spent the intervening years without crying. She had kept herself in check for a period of five years, an impossibly long time for a teenage girl.

Shido had talked with Origami a number of times before. Hung out with her any number of times. But it was in this moment that he felt like he was finally seeing her real face.

After sobbing for some time, Origami said quietly, still clinging to him, "Shido, I have to apologize to you, too."

"To me...?" He frowned. "What for?"

She pulled away from him to look up at his face as she continued. "I'm pretty sure...the feelings I had for you...weren't love."

"Huh?" He gaped at her.

"I was just...dependent on you. I molded myself to you because you happened to be there when I lost my parents. I was clinging to you to avoid looking at my own weakness. I caused so many problems for you because of these selfish feelings." She took a deep breath. "I want to apologize from the bottom of my heart."

"..." Shido exhaled slowly, and the corners of his mouth turned up. "I'm honored."

"Huh...?" Origami stared in surprise.

"At the very least, I...," he started to say, and then he stopped and tried again. "Origami, I'm honestly so glad I met you. And sure, you made some trouble for me, but...if it was those feelings that made you reach out to me now. Well, in that case, I'm actually grateful."

"Shido...," she said in a shaky voice, and tears filled her eyes once more.

Seeing these tears, he nodded slightly. "Oh right. I have to give that back to you, too."

"Give what back?" Origami cocked her head curiously to one side.

"It wasn't just your tears you entrusted me with that time," he reminded her.

"Oh…" Now she remembered. That day five years ago. The words she had spoken. The things she would give him.

"Um. I—"

"Origami."

Shido said her name as he stared into her eyes, and Origami gasped, her cheeks flushing red with embarrassment.

And then she produced an awkward but unmistakable smile.

"…!"

Origami gaped as the inky-black Astral Dress wrapped around her emitted a dazzling light and turned a snowy white.

This was the true form of the Spirit Origami Shido had seen in the original world.

The myriad of feathers floating around her turned into particles of light and disappeared.

"Shido… I…" Wrapped in the bridal Astral Dress, smile on her face, she looked almost like a real angel.

"…" He squeezed her shoulder and pulled her to him.

"Huh?" she said, baffled.

This had always been his ultimate objective. Whatever level her likability was, if he didn't do this now, he couldn't seal her Spirit power away. But he couldn't tell whether it was a sense of duty to fulfill this mission that tightened his arms around her or if it was due to his own desire.

His lips pressed against hers.

"…!" She shuddered but then quickly let her weight rest against him, like she was giving herself over to him.

In the next moment, the snowy-white Astral Dress melted away, leaving a glittering trail in the air.

"What…?" Origami pulled her lips away and opened her eyes wide at the light and her vanishing Astral Dress.

Freed from their fight against the feathers at last, the other Spirits descended to earth behind Shido, and he raised a hand slightly to signal that it was all over. The girls let out a collective sigh of relief.

"Mm!" Tohka furrowed her brow a little at the sight of a half naked Origami leaning against Shido. She sniffed indignantly as she crossed her arms. "Hmph. Well, I guess I'll allow it, but only for today, Origami."

"Hmm?" Shido smiled wryly at Tohka's attitude and then quickly realized something was slightly off. That wasn't how she'd talk to a transfer student who'd joined her class a few days earlier, but rather to a long-time friendly rival.

"Tohka, wait…" He turned to look up at her. "Do you remember Origami now?"

"Mm? What a strange thing— Mm, but I guess I do. Weird. I feel like I forgot about her until a minute ago." She twisted her head to one side, perplexed. The other Spirits had similar looks on their faces.

"So maybe…" He recalled the time when he had sealed Kotori's powers. The moment he'd kissed her, memories that had been locked away were called up through the path between them.

There was an invisible pathway between Shido and the Spirits whose powers he'd locked away. In which case, his memories of the original world had maybe been shared via that same pathway when he'd sealed Origami's powers.

"Ha-ha!" He grinned at this unexpected present. The thought flitted through his mind that not having Origami's memories might have made it easier for the other girls to build a better relationship with her, but he shook his head and tossed it away.

All of that was also Origami. Although, well, there were bound to be troubles ahead.

As Shido thought about this, Origami slowly turned her head and looked at the Spirits gathered there. "Thank you, Tohka, everyone. For fighting for me." She uttered these very un-Origami-like words.

"Wha—?!"

"Huh…?"

"What spakest thou?"

"Dubious. Have you not yet returned to your right mind?"

"Mmm, this up-front and honest Origami is soooo cute."

"Goodness, this is unusual."

Tohka and the other Spirits all (except for one) got shocked looks on their faces. But strangely, Shido wasn't surprised.

After all, the Origami standing there now had memories of both the original world and this world.

But it was apparently too unexpected for Tohka. She darted her eyes around, as if in a panic, and turned her face away. "D-don't get the wrong idea! I'm—it was that! I just helped because Shido asked me to!"

Tohka said, not being very honest, despite the fact that she had obviously been worried about Origami, too.

"Oh. Then I *don't* thank you," Origami said, rolling her eyes. "You selfish Spirit. How awful."

"Wha...?!" Tohka frowned. "That's not what you were saying a second ago!"

"Yes, it is." Origami turned her face away from her.

Shido couldn't help but smile at this. There were indeed bound to be troubles ahead.

Epilogue
Origami Tobiichi

November 14. Shido stared at the classroom door from where he sat at his desk. Morning homeroom was going to start in another five minutes or so. Every so often, the door opened, and his classmates entered.

"…"

This was the general time at which people arrived at school, so it was only natural that the door would be opening frequently. But Shido's eyebrows jumped every time nonetheless.

The reason was simple. It had been three days since he'd sealed Origami's Spirit powers at the park on the plateau. Today, now that Ratatoskr had finished its battery of examinations, Origami would be coming back to school at last.

Although the Spirits had their fair share of injuries, as did Kotori and her crew, they had all survived somehow. And given the fact that they had been up against such a tremendously powerful inverted Spirit, they had gotten off lucky. Well, Kotori was in a thoroughly foul mood now that her precious *Fraxinus* had been battered and beaten, however.

"Hmm." He fidgeted in his chair, sighed, and scratched his cheek. He knew there was no need to be so nervous. But after the sealing, a dispatched member of Ratatoskr had taken Origami not to the seriously damaged *Fraxinus* but to an underground facility owned by the organization, so Shido hadn't seen her at all since then.

Which would mean that today would be the first time he'd really be talking with the Origami who had memories of both this world and the original world. More than anything else—

"…" He touched his lips silently.

Yes. This was the biggest thing bothering him. Despite the fact that it had been necessary to lock her powers away, a person wouldn't normally go kissing someone immediately after they told you the feelings they had for you were not love. Origami hadn't said anything at the time, but Shido was still feeling supremely awkward about it.

"Shido, is Origami still not here?" Tohka said abruptly, eyeing the door the same as he was, with her arms crossed.

It appeared that his guess had indeed been correct, and memories of the original world had been shared with the Spirits through the pathway that opened when he sealed Origami's powers. Ever since that day, Tohka and the rest of them knew all there was to know about Origami. All of them knew things that hadn't happened in *this* world. It was sort of a strange feeling.

But it seemed that everything wasn't quite back to the way it had been.

"Tohka," he said with a smile, propping his chin up in his hands. "Looks like you're calling her Origami now, huh?"

Her eyes flew open, and she hurried to respond, "Mm. I-it's no big deal. I just sort of felt like it." Arms still crossed, she averted her eyes.

Tohka used to call Origami by her full name, Origami Tobiichi. He had no idea what had changed inside her, but personally, he felt like it wasn't a bad development.

"Hmm. Origami has yet to appear then?"

"Assent. Did we come too soon?"

He heard voices from behind and looked back to find the Yamai sisters standing there, pointlessly striking poses.

"Kaguya. Yuzuru," he said. "What's with the posing? And you two are in Class Three. What're you doing here?"

Kaguya threw a hand up in front of her face to peer at him from between her fingers. "Keh-keh. So you are curious. We heard word that the dunce has at last completed the examinations and shall be returning. We would offer our certain gratitude for her actions in the original world!" she said, cackling, as a wicked smile crossed her face.

Now that she mentioned it, she and the others had been mercilessly trounced by the Spirit Origami in the original world. And Kaguya was apparently holding a grudge. It seemed that giving them these memories of the original world hadn't been an entirely good thing.

"Are you planning to exact revenge on Origami, too, Yuzuru?" He turned his eyes toward the other sister as he grinned wryly at Kaguya tenting her fingers together in anticipation of Origami.

But Yuzuru, in contrast, shook her head vigorously. "Negation. Yuzuru is not particularly bothered about that. I'm happier that Origami reconsidered her position on Spirits."

"Hey!" Kaguya erupted indignantly. "You're making me look super petty!"

Well, their words might have been different, but he expected that they both wanted to welcome Origami back. As he watched them argue, he sighed and turned his eyes to the doorway once more.

"Still, though. She's pretty late. Homeroom's going to—," he started to say and then stopped.

The door opened, and in came Origami.

"Origami—" His eyes immediately grew as wide as saucers at the sight of her. Origami had cut her long hair so that it grazed her shoulders, making her transformation into the Origami that Shido knew complete.

Tohka and the Yamai sisters also gaped at the new/old Origami, but they quickly recovered.

"Mm. So you came, Origami!"

"Keh-keh! The nerve! I shall commend you only on your foolhardiness!"

Tohka and Kaguya faced Origami as if steeling themselves.

"Morning, everyone," Origami said, without a hint of malice on her face, leaving Tohka and Kaguya to stammer and gape, as if the wind had been taken out of their sails.

Only Yuzuru responded. "Reply. Good morning, Master Origami."

"Origami, you…," Shido started to say and stopped again after realizing that what he had been about to say was not what he *should* say.

So instead he said, in his usual tone, his usual voice, "Morning, Origami." Words he thought for a while that he would never get to say again.

Origami smiled and nodded and then slowly walked toward him. And then stopped next to the desk where he was seated.

"Mm-hmm. Morning," she said one more time, staring into his eyes.

Looking at her face, Shido was overcome by deep emotion. Her hair was indeed short now, and her overall appearance once again matched the Origami he used to know. But perhaps because she had memories of this world, or perhaps because her thinking about the Spirits had changed, he got the feeling that the expression on her face and the general air about her had noticeably softened.

Tohka and the others seemed to pick up on this, too. They looked slightly perplexed at how to react to her. But they'd get used to it soon enough.

Tohka and the Spirits were there, Origami was there. Shido felt himself tearing up at this sight he'd seen any number of times in the original world.

"Mm? You okay, Shido?" Tohka asked, peering into his face.

"Oh. Yeah. It's nothing," he said, faux-casually, and was about to wipe away the tears with the back of his hand when Origami grabbed his wrist.

"Shido," she said. "If you're wiping tears away, then here."

"O-oh. Thanks." He reached out toward her. But she was not offering him anything along the lines of a handkerchief or a hand towel. "Origami? What do you mean by—?"

Suddenly, his head was yanked forward, and his field of view went black.

"…?!"

Slight moisture touched his cheeks, followed by the scent of soap and sweat mixed together, tickling his nostrils. A heartbeat later, he realized his head had been pulled into Origami's skirt.

"…!" He gasped and tried to escape, but Origami did not release the hold she had on the back of his head. In fact, the more he struggled, the more his face was pressed up against her abdomen. "Nnn! Hnnnnngh!"

"Wh-what are you *doing*?!" Tohka's panicked voice rang out, and Origami's hold was released at last.

When he finally returned to a place of light, he was panting heavily, his eyes darting around. "Haaah, haaah… Haaah…!"

"Origami! Why'd you do that?!" Tohka shouted.

"I was just wiping his tears away," Origami stated flatly.

"Don't give me that! H-how was *that* wiping anything?!"

Origami flipped her skirt up without any hesitation whatsoever.

"Wha…?!" Shido gasped. But beneath her skirt were not underpants but a navy-blue school swimsuit.

"Excellent water absorption," she said.

"No, wait. But." He stared at her blankly. "Why would you…? It's already November. We don't have lessons in the pool anymore?"

"I thought you would want to continue what we started." She pulled a headband with dog ears on it, a tail, and a leather collar from her bag.

The other people in their class began to whisper at the array of unusual items.

"Uhhh. What is Tobiichi doing?"

"What did she get up to while she was out sick?"

"That reminds me. A friend of mine saw Itsuka and Tobiichi walking together…"

"For real? She's a rising star, though. She raced all the way up to number one in the rankings of girls you'd want to date on the first day she transferred in here?!"

"But you know, it's Itsuka and all."

"Ohh."

He heard bits and pieces of the conversations around them. And although he couldn't catch the full sentences, he also heard disturbing words like "confinement," "compulsion," and "training" being bandied about.

But maybe this was inevitable. The Spirits might have remembered the original world, but his classmates couldn't, not when there was no pathway between him and them. All they knew was the serious Origami from before she'd been absent.

"Uh. Um. Origami?" he said nervously. "There are a lot of people here, so maybe you shouldn't really say stuff like—"

"No need for concern," she replied and leaned in close to him.

"Ngah!" he yelped.

"H-hey!" Tohka cried out, and the rest of the class started chattering as one. Some of them even turned their cell phone cameras toward Shido and Origami.

However, Origami spoke with absolute calm. "It's best to inform them as soon as possible of our relationship, Shido. This way, no one else will come sniffing around."

"Y-you get away from Shido, Origami!" Tohka shouted, and Origami turned quiet eyes on her.

"It is true that I have stopped viewing Spirits as targets for absolute annihilation," she said. "However, I will not let you have Shido. As long as you follow him around, you are still my enemy."

"I could say the same thing!" Tohka shrieked, waving her arms about. "Now get away from Shido right this second!"

But Origami stayed pressed against him with a cool look on her face.

"Uh. Um… Tobiichi?" he said in a tiny voice, feeling the itch of the gazes around him. There was one thing he needed to check on with her.

"What?"

"Oh. Uh. If my memory serves," he said, sweat beading on his forehead. "When all that happened, didn't you say that your feelings for me weren't love?"

She nodded firmly. "I did."

"So, umm. Then what is all this about?" he said, trying to distance himself from her under the stares they were collecting. This was no different from the original world. In fact, he felt like things had even escalated slightly.

She looked at him coolly. "What I've felt for you up until now was not love; it was dependence."

"R-right." He nodded.

"True love begins now."

"…" He felt dizzy. This wasn't love; it was dependence. He felt almost like it had been the great Demon King making this declaration.

In the middle of this commotion, the bell to signal the start of homeroom rang.

Perfect timing. Shido peeled Origami off him and said in a voice loud enough for everyone to hear, "C-come on! Homeroom's starting! Tohka, Origami, sit down. Kaguya, Yuzuru, go back to your own class!"

"M-mm…"

"…"

"Hmph. If we must. We shall return at the break!"

"Retreat. At a later time, then. Master Origami, let us speak again."

Tohka and Origami laid down their arms, and the Yamai sisters returned to Class 3. Perhaps realizing this was the end of the spectacle, the rest of his classmates also marched back to their desks.

"Haaah." Shido let out a long sigh as he snuck a glance at Origami. Because she had appeared in such an unexpected way, he'd missed his chance to say it before. "Origami?"

"What?"

"Umm. So like. Thanks for hearing my voice that day. I'm glad you came back to me. It's uh… I'm relieved. That you're here in class like normal… It might be difficult to make friends with the Spirits right away, but I just know you'll manage to do okay with it. So… Uhhh." Even though he'd pictured their reunion so clearly yesterday, when it was actually happening, he couldn't manage to get the words out. He scratched his head. "Aah, I'll stop. We can talk about the hard stuff later. At any rate…"

He lifted his face and looked into her eyes.

"I'm looking forward to what comes next."

"Mm-hmm," Origami replied with a smile.

Afterword

Hello. My favorite Rewarder is Nenesu Totoru. This is Koushi Tachibana. I'm bringing you *Date A Live*, Vol. 11: *Devil Tobiichi*. What did you think? I do hope you enjoyed it.

It's the Devil here, the Devil. A complete one-eighty from Volume 10's Angel Tobiichi, D-E-V-I-L. Meaning that Origami's ears are hell ears. There's nothing but the smell of danger here.

And well, it is rather sudden, but who is this beautiful girl on the cover? Isn't she extremely cute? Isn't that Devil smile like that of an Angel? For a second, I thought it was Origami, but her hair is too long for it to be Origami. But she really does look just like Origami. And this is when I think, it has to be that. It's Origami's little sister, Irogami. I never dreamed that this snippet from Volume 2 would be picked up in a place like this. This hasn't happened since Rodriguez (*Soukyuu no Karma* volumes one through eight, on sale now).

As another possibility, there could also be Origami's daughter, Chiyogami. She's a beautiful girl who takes after her mother. Or maybe it's a new arrival, Origami's cousin Udagami, or her second cousin Kiraragami, or there's also the possibility of Kotakushi or Kentoshi, who used to live near Origami's house, or Atsude-matte-shi. No. That's not possible.

All jokes aside, this is a shocking metamorphosis for Origami. There's no doubt about it. Shido did say that he prefers girls with long hair. Or it goes without Shido saying it; Origami has collected that data. And then in a single day, she grows her hair out. This is Origami we're talking about, after all.

Leaving that for now, this volume has, yet again, a special structure.

In fact, we did this once before as well. Yes, the usual splash page illustration in each volume… Take a look, hmm? Tsunako did magnificent work there. Those of you who haven't already seen it, please dig into the main story right away.

Also, I'm sure you're all aware of this already, but there is going to be a theatrical version of this very *Date A Live*! Whoo-hoo! Clap-clap! A feature-length film. A film, friends. Amazing, hmm? It's Tohka's silver screen debut. I had thought it would be so nice if the Natsumi and Origami arcs also made it into animation, but a feature film was beyond my expectations.

On top of that, it will not be a straight adaptation of the books, but rather an original story. I'm sure there will be more updates to come, so please look forward to that!

Now then, once more, this book made it to the shelves with the support of so many people. Illustrator Tsunako, Little Miss Eye Patch in the front pages is unbearably cute. My editor and everyone in the editorial department, the designer, everyone in sales and logistics, bookshop clerks, and all the readers who picked up this book, thank you so much.

Next up is the short story collection *Date A Live: Encore 3*, followed by the publication of *Date A Live*, Vol. 12.

All right, then. I look forward to meeting you again.

Koushi Tachibana
August 2014